CW00552213

RAYMOND FRIEL is a Scottish scree
has two feature film credits: *The*
Bloom and *Botched* with Stephen Dorff. Both of these films were released in cinemas in the UK and distributed worldwide.

Friel has worked on a variety of other film and television projects with the UK Film Council, Scottish Screen, Creative Scotland, Shine Entertainment, Channel 4 and the BBC.

His play, *Moriarty Is Crying*, won the Willy Russell Award for New Writing and was performed at the Edinburgh Festival and the Citizens Theatre in Glasgow.

Friel also writes and directs a live comedy sketch show that has featured in the Glasgow Comedy Festival and played to sell out crowds.

He lives with his wife and two children, Rémy and Etienne. His Jack Russells, Stubby and Rigsby, feel the book could have done with a bit more rabbit chasing and a lot less talking.

To Linda,

If you buy the next one I'll set you
up with Orlando Bloom!

Animal Lover

Many Thanks

Raymond Friel

RAYMOND FRIEL

Luath Press Limited
EDINBURGH
www.luath.co.uk

First published 2013

ISBN: 978-1-908373-72-4

The paper used in this book is recyclable. It is made from
low chlorine pulps produced in a low energy, low emissions manner
from renewable forests.

The publishers acknowledge the support of

ALBA | CHRUTHACHAIL

towards the publication of this volume.

Printed and bound by
Bell & Bain Ltd., Glasgow

Typeset in 10.5 point Sabon
by 3btype.com

For Babeth,
without you
there is no story.

I

Tonight. Tonight is all that matters. Everything else, all this, neon lights and the smell of disinfectant and dead chickens, don't let it get to you. Baked beans not a problem. On the shelf they go. Super Danny: by day a quiet Morrisons grocery worker but by night... I laugh but have to pretend I'm coughing as Joanne glances up at me. The last thing I need is people here thinking I'm odd.

    —What you laughing at?

    —Nothing.

She stares at me.

    —Share the joke Danny.

    —I was coughing, honestly.

Joanne continues to stare at me as the corners of her mouth droop. How old is she? Seventeen? Shouldn't she be harder than this?

    —I bet if it was someone else you'd tell them. Nobody likes
      me here. You were probably laughing at me.

She turns back to the case of baked beans. Brilliant. I feel guilty. She sniffs, her face hidden. Jesus Christ. She's crying. It is 7.05am, I've been awake for an hour, at work for five minutes and already experiencing uncomfortable moment of the day number one. Best just to ignore it and continue working. Katie appears at the end of the aisle with a metal cage for the used cardboard boxes heading our way. Joanne's shoulders shake slightly, her long black Goth hair dangling. You don't need to say anything Danny, you really don't.

—Joanne, I wasn't laughing. At anything, especially not you. It's this cough, seriously, I think I'm coming down with something… Please, don't cry.

Poor kid. I remember seventeen. I remember everything. Twenty-two and already I have to fight my memories just to get up in the morning. By the time I'm thirty I may well be bed bound.

—Who's crying? Joanne says.

She turns to me, tears definitely *not* streaming down her face.

—What's going on? Katie says.

Uh-oh. There has been a misjudgement.

—Danny's got a joke but he's not telling, Joanne says.

Oh shit, the manager, Mark, is heading our way. This has got to be dealt with quickly or an escalation is inevitable.

—There's no joke Katie. Forget it.

—C'mon Danny, tell us, Katie says.

But she's not going to push it. God bless you Katie. Used to like her a lot when I thought it was just me she found funny then realised she laughed at anything and felt cheated. Then disliked her. Mark arrives, smiling at the girls but not at me, surprise surprise.

—What are your demands? he says.

Nobody says anything but I can guess yours, ya sleazy bastard. He must be almost forty and yet spends every works night out trying to fire into the teenage lassies.

—Oh sorry, I thought you were on strike, Mark says, —but if you're not on strike get back to work.

He laughs but nobody joins in. Wanker. Still, at least it took the focus away from me.

—Danny's got a joke he was just about to tell us, Joanne says. —We'll get back to work once he has.

Bitch.

—On you go then, Mark says, —and afterwards I've got a belter that'll blow yours out of the water.

—Let's hear it Danny, Katie says.

—Yeah, says Joanne.

Quick glance at the clock. 7.07am and uncomfortable moment of the day number two is already upon us. One every two minutes, thirty an hour. Almost 1500 a day. That's a lot of uncomfortable moments. Time to trawl through Christmas cracker joke memory... Got one.

—In Alaska they have a lottery only for the Eskimos.

Joanne sniffs again and this time I see her face when she does so. Interesting, it's a sign of anger, not pain.

—Oh great, a racist joke. Pathetic. Why don't you just change your name to Jim Davidson? she says.

—So what if he likes Jim Davidson? says Mark.

No no no. This isn't right. I don't want Mark or Jim Davidson on my side.

—It's not racist –

—I think you can make jokes about anything as long as it's funny, Katie says.

—So you'd laugh at a rape or an abortion joke? Joanne says.

Katie doesn't answer, beaten.

—You won't like my one then, Mark says.

He laughs, again on his own.

    —If you don't want to hear it that's fine, I say.

    —Just hurry up and finish it, Joanne says.

    —Ok then. In Alaska they have a lottery only for the Eskimos.

    —And you a vegetarian.

    —What's that got to do with it?

Joanne rolls her eyes as if it's so obvious she doesn't need to answer. This girl is as hard as nails. No wonder. She's seventeen. Those bastards think they're bullet proof.

    —I've got a couple of Jim Davidson DVDs you can borrow if you like, Mark says.

    —No thanks. I think Jim Davidson is a cunt. Same with the people that like him.

Perhaps overstepped the mark there. Mark. My boss. I have just called a cunt. Uncomfortable moment number three arrived quicker than I thought.

    —Just trying to be friendly, Mark says.

And looks at me with hate. If he didn't particularly care for me in the general way that a certain type of man dislikes every other guy who's younger or slimmer or just has anything that he might be jealous of before we have now graduated to a more personal level of enmity, bona fide *enemies*. He will try to get me at some point. Something to think about. At least I've not offended Katie.

    —I don't like that word, Katie says.

    —What word? I say.

    —The C-word. The one you just used.

Clean sweep. Christ. There is a really bad vibe coming from

these three fuckers and as if they can sense that there is cama-
raderie to be had they move closer together.

—Joke now. Then back to work. I mean it, Mark says.
That was said as a threat.

—In Alaska they have a lottery only for the Eskimos.
They stare at me. Bad crowd.

—You have to be Inuit to win it.

Joanne shakes her head and bends down to the cans at her feet.
Katie turns and walks back down the aisle, the metal cage in
tow, smiling at a bloke who asks her where the tinned tomatoes
are but not stopping to answer him. Mark lingers and gives me
a smile but we both know what's behind it.

Super Danny.

2

Keep it together keep it together keep it together. You're the leader, they look up to you. Christ it's tight in here, borderline claustrophobia kicking in, try not to think about it. Jesus. Fuckin' buried alive. At least we're moving. As long as we're moving I'm ok.

—Danny, can we stop for a bit?

Paul again. If I didn't know better I'd think he didn't want to be here.

—No we can't. This isn't a walk in the park man!

—I know but I can feel a cramp coming on –

—Enough. Move yer arse.

Quick glance over at Shona, how did she feel I handled that? Can't really tell in this light. In this dark. So cramped in here. Every time her right arm moves as she crawls forward it brushes against me and I find myself looking forward to each moment of accidental contact.

—Ow!

—Sorry Danny. I didn't realise my elbow was that close, she says.

—It's ok. It didn't hurt.

Another bruise probably. I can take it. I am a man. Best check on Seb, don't like leaving anyone out.

—How's Seb?

—Hundred per cent, he says.

A voice from the darkness. Good lad. I can always trust Seb. There it is! Ya fuckin' beauty. Light at the end of the tunnel. Something to aim for. God, I never thought it was true but it's like what they say, the pounding of the blood in my veins is deafening.

—Stop making that noise Paul, Shona says.

—I told you, I've got cramp. I'm having to drag my leg.

What was I thinking that the noise was my blood? I may be freaking out. Don't let it show.

—Ya fuckin' idiot Paul! You trying to get us caught ya fuckin' prick!

I didn't mean to say that. I don't even really swear. Not like some. Cunt word cunt word. Mostly hear them on buses.

—What now Danny? Shona asks.

Time to focus. I motion at them to be quiet and shuffle to the grate at the end of the air vent. And look through. Bastards. Bastards. Bastards. How much money do these fuckers need? No humans but a lot of life. Like BUPA except instead of beds there are cages. Maybe about twenty in all each holding at least one dog, some two or three. Computer station in the middle, that's where the keys should be. Time to do some good.

—You can come up, I say. -There's no one here. But be quiet. Shona squeezes against me, Seb behind us, Paul keeping his distance at the back.

—Okay, military operation here ladies and gentlemen, I say. -I know they're all wankers but let's have a SAS type attitude –

Paul sneezes.

—You fuckin' did that on purpose!

—I didn't! It's all the dust in here. I have allergies y'know.

—Oh… Sorry. But try to be quiet, eh? Bravo Two Zero mentality.

—That was all bullshit, Seb whispers.

—What?

—Bravo Two Zero. I saw a programme on Channel 4. They did nothing apart from kill a few conscripts and then surrender. Murdering shitbags really.

—Yeah, I saw that as well, Shona says.

This is getting away from me. What was I thinking pretending to be the SAS? Apart from everything else they're the enemy, tools of an animal exploiting corporate elite. Wouldn't be surprised if a few of them have tailed me in the past. That old guy outside the B&Q, something funny was going on there and it wasn't just in my head.

—Forget the SAS but let's be professional, that's all I was meaning. Actually, all I was really meaning was gonna not sneeze again Paul.

—It's not my fault. It's my membranes.

Ignore him and push the grate but it's stuck. Shit. I move round and give it a kick. Fuck, too hard. It flies off and crashes against the floor. The dogs start to bark and I can't help myself. I freeze. Shona tugs at me.

—Danny?

—*Danny?*

The dogs are quieting down. I'm coming back… I'm back.

—Yeah, sorry, what?

—Paul's run away, she says.

—Paul! Get back here!

I can hear my voice echoing down the duct. I may have frozen but at least I didn't run. Paul returns, can't see his face but his shuffle sounds guilty.

—Where the hell do you think you were going?

He shrinks. I'll let him off this time.

—Ok, I say. –I'll go first. Give me some space.

They back out my way so that I can lower myself out of the duct. My legs go first and dangle in the open air, shit, this isn't good, I didn't realise we were so high up, I'm gonna fall –

—Ah! Fuck!

That's it, my leg's broke. No, wait a second, the pain's spiked and then disappeared. I'm alright. I must have hit that table on my way down. Get my bearings. I'm in the middle of an animal vivisection lab. Middle of an animal vivisection lab. *We are really fucking doing this!* This probably *is* a bit like the SAS. Shona pokes her head out. She looks worried for me. Tonight is getting better and better.

—Danny, you ok? she says.

I give her the thumbs up though I expect I'll be limping tomorrow.

—Who's next?

Shona wriggles herself out of the duct and I make sure I'm there to catch her. Temptation to hold her for too long makes me hold her not long enough and I almost drop her.

—Sorry.

—No worries, she says.

And leaves my side, distracted by the animals. Seb lowers himself and this time there's no mistake. With the blond fringe and that bandana wrapped around the lower part of his face I can only see his eyes. He loves that bandana, I can't ever remember him being without it.

—Thanks, he says.

And joins Shona at the cages.

—Ok Paul, your turn.

Paul pokes his head out and lingers there.

—What's the problem? I say.

He sneezes again but now that I can see his face something about the action doesn't seem right. Is he faking?

—I was thinking that we could maybe do with a lookout? Paul says.

—Get down here.

He screws his face up and glances back the way we came before coming to a decision and lurching forward, holding his arms out towards me.

—No, the other way –

But it's too late. He slides out and I do my best but he still lands on his head. That looked painful. Best not give him the chance to moan though. No sympathy for victims.

—On your feet soldier, I say.

And pull him up. I look over and see Shona kneeling down at a cage, a small pink tongue licking her fingers through the mesh. I could do with some of that action myself and join her. The dogs are mostly fully grown but still puppies, between six months and a year, but a couple are only a few weeks old. They come to the front of the cages wagging their tails. Jesus Christ. To think that they're still looking for human company after all we've done to them. The knot in my stomach is back. This isn't fun. I feel like burning this hellhole to the ground.

—Who's a good boy! Shona says.

But her voice is cracking. Please don't cry, if you do you'll set me off.

—What we waiting for then? Paul says.

He's still standing where he fell. I pull myself away from the dogs and get back on track.

—You're right, I say. –This is a breakout not a get together.

—Danny, I think this one likes me! Shona says.

I'm at the computer station busy going through the drawers with Seb but look up and smile at her anyway.

—They'll like us a helluva lot more once we've rescued them.

—Can we please hurry the fuck up! Paul says.

He's moved to the door trying to listen for any sign of security, nervously holding his crotch. He must be terrified. Good. His cowardice is making me brave. Could always tell him to relax, that would make me feel even calmer. What's that noise? No, oh God she is. Shona is crying, and not just a whimper either.

—Jesus fucking Christ, that's all we need, Paul says.

—Leave her alone, I say. –Has anybody got a hankie?

—Got them!

Seb holds up the keys and hands them to me. Check on Shona. She's got the tears under control. Back to the cages and this time not to play. As I unlock the doors the dogs hang back but not for long. By the time I've opened half of them the dogs are out, sniffing each other and jumping up at Seb and Shona.

—It's gonna be ok, Shona says to a couple of dogs rolling on their backs at her feet.

Now to release the others and they're desperate to be free, sensing that good times are to be had. Seb is laughing and on his knees playing with one of the dogs. Shona's picked up a puppy and is hugging it tight. The dogs are getting more and more excited. This could get out of hand. Time to take control.

—Right everyone, listen up, I say. –We know what we've got to do.

Well that didn't work. Shona and Seb are still mucking about with the animals. I can't help myself and pat the dog nearest to me. It looks up and wags its tail. I bet the bastards haven't even named them. Ok, you're Norman.

—Danny! It's time to go! Paul says.

—Yeah. I know. Don't tell me that. Shona, Seb, that's enough. Come on.

They look over and I open my bag and start flinging the leads to them.

—Let's get the dogs under control and then we're gone.

I try to get a hold of Norman but he runs away, thinking it's a game.

—Norman, get back here!

I start chasing him.

—Danny, I don't believe in leads, Shona says.

I stop running after Norman.

—What?

She shrugs.

—I don't believe in leads.

—Shona, please. This isn't the time.

—I know, it's just we're here to free them and then we're putting chains round their necks? It doesn't make sense.

Seb raises his hand.

—I don't believe in leads either.

—We've been through this, I say. —The ends justify the means. It'll be a lot easier getting them out if we've got them on leads. Once we're out you can do whatever the hell you want with them.

—I don't want to *do* anything with them, Shona says.

—I didn't mean it like that –

—Hey genius, Paul says.

I look over. He's caught a dog and is holding the lead at its neck.

—They don't have collars. What we gonna do now?

I open my mouth but say nothing. There's always something. There's always bloody something. Paul perks up.

—Maybe we should just forget about it, he says.

—We can't. Danny, tell him, Shona says.

Christ, she really does think I'm the leader. Don't let her down.

—There's no two ways about it. We ain't leaving the dogs behind, I say.

Shona smiles and Seb gives a clenched fist salute.

—So how we gonna get them out then? Paul says.

—I'll show you.

I finally manage to grab Norman and climb onto the table near the vent. I place him at the opening. He takes one nervous look at the dark tunnel and then faces me. Come on Norman, don't let me down.

—On you go, you know what's out there? Liberty, freedom... fucking cats.

Norman's not going anywhere. He tries to lick my face. Shit.

—They're never gonna go in the vent unless we drag them and we can't do that because they don't have any collars! Paul shouts.

—He's got a point, Seb says. —Maybe we'd be able to rescue one each but the others would never follow.

—Yeah, good idea Seb, Paul says. —We'll take one each. At least then we're rescuing four of them. Danny, c'mon, let's do it.

At the edge of my vision I can feel her staring at me. That's a worry, because if I can sense her gaze on me, does that mean she's noticed when I stare at her when I think she's not looking?

—No, I said we're getting them all out and that's what we're gonna do.

I head for the door to the lab.

—Danny, we can't go that way, it might be alarmed, Paul says.

Turn and give him (but really her) a little crooked smile.

—Yeah, and it might not be.

I try the handle. The alarm goes off. **WAAAAAA!** Fuck me but that's loud. Shitshitshitshit. And now the dogs are barking.

—I fuckin' told you that was going to happen!

—Shut up Paul. Just let me think...

Can't tell if he hears me though because there's so much other noise. Beginning to freeze up again. Rabbit in the headlights time. I'm aware of Paul scrabbling on top of the table and trying to pull himself into the air vent but he's not strong enough and falls to the floor, immediately getting to his feet and trying again.

—Somebody help me up! he shouts.

We all ignore him.

—Danny, we should hide, Seb says.

That did the trick. I'm back in the zone. Good lad Seb. Time for me (the leader) to take control again, some new stratagem to impress my fellows and confound my foes.

—Everyone! Hide! Fuckin' anywhere!

I grab the handle to a cupboard close to me. There's enough space for two. Shona hasn't moved, standing in the middle of the room still holding the puppy.

—Shona! Here!

She follows me in and as I close the door I can see Seb dragging Paul into a similar cupboard opposite us. Shona moves closer to me, squeezing in so that the door can close completely. Click. It does, but I can still see through the slits in the wood. The dogs

are having a great time, Norman's on the table with the comput-
ers knocking over folders. That's my boy, doing his bit against
the machine. Someone's coming. The door to the lab opens.
   —Fuckin' hell!
A man's voice.
   —How'd they get out? says another.
Security guards. Shit. Pretend to be invisible Danny. Become
one with the cupboard. Should I tell Shona to pretend to be
invisible? I mouth at her but she's too busy looking after the
puppy. Forget it, I'll just pretend for her. Ok, here it goes. I am
not here. What's that scrabbling? Oh no. Norman's off the table
and trying to get into the cupboard. Fuck off Norman! I blank
him and luckily he gets bored and goes looking for his mates.
The two security guards round up the dogs and put them back
in their cages one at a time. Every time they catch a dog Shona
winces. She looks at me. I shake my head, I want to reassure
her, tell her not to worry, that I'm here and I won't let them get
away with it, but it seems forced, even to me. She presses herself
against the wall and her long auburn hair touches my face. I
can't help myself and take a deep breath, trying to inhale not
just the smell but everything about her. Is this how it starts? You
begin by smelling a girl's hair and then end up five years later
in a strange woman's bedroom trying to find a soiled pair of
knickers for the next nostril hit? Did Fred West start this way?
Stop it Danny. It's perfectly normal to want to smell a girl's hair.
You're not a pervert. Stay switched on, you can worry about
being a deviant later. Norman is the last to be caught and I feel
a bit of pride as he gives the security guards the run-a-round.
They're out of breath and sit for a minute. Security guards.
They're all fat bastards.

—You ready to go?

The other nods. They leave. We stay. This is the closest I've ever been to her. Y'know Danny you could always – *Christ!* Where did that thought come from? What? Here? Now? The adrenaline must be making me drunk cause there's no way normally –

—Do you want to go out with me? To the pictures or something? I say.

There it is. Out in the open. She straightens and slowly turns her head to face me. I think I'm smiling at her but it could just be the anxiety twisting my face. It probably looks like a leer, oh God, she might think this whole operation was a ploy to rub myself up against her in a cupboard. Fred West *could* have started this way. She nods and smiles back at me. She fucking nodded!

—But after we're done here, she says.

—Oh yeah. Obviously. You can choose the film if you like.

I beam at her. Temptation to say something stupid but this time I'm gonna keep my mouth shut.

—Is that why you've been staring at me? she says.

—What? Have I been staring at you?

—When you think I'm not looking, she says.

—Sorry.

I can feel myself go red. She rubs her nose against the puppy still in her arms, her turn to look embarrassed.

—Don't be sorry. I've been hoping you'd ask me out for ages.

—Really? Well, I've just been waiting for the perfect moment. Result. First laugh of the relationship. We're only an inch or two apart. Fucking hell. I could be on for a snog. The sound of the door reopening makes me pull back and check what's going on. The security guards have returned and are at the alarm.

—You always forget to reset it, one of them says.

—I'm doing it now, amn't I? the other answers.

—Get a move on, this is supposed to be our break.

I strain my eyes. Holy shit, I can see what he's doing, see the actual numbers he's punching in. One, eight, six, eight, four, four, seven, two. Use your head Danny. I know how we can do this. I'm gonna get us out of here. All I have to do is remember. One, eight, six, eight, four, four, seven, two. One, eight, six, eight, four, four, seven, two. There's a beep and it's done and as the guards head out the door I keep mouthing the numbers to make them stick. Shona taps me on the shoulder.

—What you doing?

—I saw it. I saw the fuckin' code. But I need help. One, eight, six, eight, four, four, seven, two, I say. –You remember the first two numbers. One and eight, got it? That's you.

—One and eight no problem, she says.

But looks at me funny, I don't think she gets it. We're out of the cupboard and my mind is on fire. One, eight, six, eight, four, four, seven, two. There's a voice in my head flinging random numbers at me. Why would my own brain do that? 'Two' 'two' 'six' 'seven' 'six' 'five' 'two'. Where the hell did that come from? Shit. That's the phone number of the house I lived in when I was five. Concentrate Danny. One, eight, six, eight, four, four, seven, two. They're the only numbers that exist on the planet. Paul bursts from the cupboard he was hiding in, Seb after him.

—It didn't mean anything. Forget about it, Seb says to Paul. Even though my mind is preoccupied I can sense something is going on. For starter's Seb's bandana is down. God he looks young. Paul is distraught.

—Just stay away from me, Paul says.

He looks close to tears. What the hell went on in there? Not your problem. Concentrate. One, eight, six, eight, four, four, seven, two.

—Danny. I've been violated. I want to go home, Paul says.
No time for that.

—I know the fucking alarm code! I say —I saw the security guard do it. Are you listening to me? One, eight, six, eight, four, four, seven, two! Got that? Everybody memorise the numbers I give them. Shona you remember what you are?

—One and eight.

—Perfect. Seb, six and eight. Ok?

He nods, pulling the scarf back over his face and looking guilty. What the fuck happened in that cupboard?

—Paul. Four and four. Remember those numbers like your life depends on it.

—I'm not really in the mood for this –

—Just remember the fuckin' numbers, alright?

—Ok ok. Four four. No big deal.

—And I'll do the rest. The guards are on a break. We got to move fast.

When we unlock the cages the dogs come bounding out but this time we're all business. I can hear Paul, Seb and Shona murmuring their numbers to themselves. As if remembering two numbers is hard. They should try the whole list. Eight. Now that's hard. I'm the leader, I guess remembering the most numbers comes with the territory. Paul isn't helping, staring into space but I'm not gonna shout at him. Something bad occurred and even though I want to know, part of me doesn't. Seb sees me looking at him.

—Paul was about to sneeze again... So I kissed him to take his mind off it. It's not like we're dating or anything.

Oh fuck. What happened between me and Shona seemed special and spontaneous at the time but maybe that's just what happens to everybody when they get in a cupboard with someone else? Thank God I was with her but the experience has already been cheapened. Shona's not let go of the puppy but that's ok I guess, I've got my eye on Norman, I'm busting that bugger out of here if it's the last thing I do. The dogs are free and I head to the door. There's the panel and the alarm system. Mission Impossible, that's what they said. Well, they hadn't heard of me.

—Shona you're first.

—One and eight.

I punch it in.

—Forty-four, says Paul.

I almost do it.

—What you up to Paul? Seb was next. Fuckssake.

—Six and eight.

—Thank you Seb. Now it's your turn Paul.

—You want me to say it again?

—Don't bother. Forty-four. Jesus.

What is that guy's problem? Oh yes. Life can change for the better or the worse in the cupboard, just don't go in unless you're willing to take the consequences. Next week, the toilet. Stop it Danny. Stay in the moment. I look at the LCD display in front of me. They're all waiting for the final numbers and then we can go. We can go. We can all go home. I stare at it some more. Shit.

—Have you forgotten the numbers? Paul says.

—No of course not... I'm just thinking.

—What you thinking about?

—Please Paul, not now.

But he's not letting up.

—Cause if you've forgotten the numbers we're better just going out the way we came in. We'll rescue the dogs another time.

Shona holds the puppy tighter to her chest and her eyes home in on mine. We'll never be in this position again, it's a miracle we've come this far as it is. The first number was definitely seven. I know that. That's safe. It's the last number. The final one. Is it four? Could be. No. Definitely not. It's gone. I'm too scared to even have a pet because of my bastard landlord and I thought I could do this? Oh fuck. Fuck. Fuck it. I stab the number three on the panel. The alarm goes off as I pull the door open.

—*Run!*

The corridor's long and I got no idea where we're going but at least we're moving and the dogs are with us. I'm at the front but I don't think it counts as leading when you're lost. End of the corridor, sliding and almost falling but manage to keep my feet. There they are, the security guards.

—Other way!

I turn and somebody bangs into me, Seb maybe, but it doesn't matter cause I'm back up and running as fast as I can. Stairs. I'm already at the top of the first flight before I realise what I'm doing and even though I've seen *Scream* and know they can only lead to a dead end it makes so much sense and it's too late to change my mind anyway and fuck it I just keep on going up the stairs up the stairs up the stairs. Paul's overtaken me and Seb is behind him. Shona's level and I don't know why but I try to smile at her, to reassure her again, but she isn't looking at me and who I am kidding, anyway? Round a corner and bang into Seb and Paul, fucking Keystone Cops routine. It wasn't supposed to be like this.

—There's no more stairs Danny, Paul says.

Seb doesn't say anything, just stands there. Is he frightened? Can't tell cause his bandana's pulled right over his face. He's not frightened. Not Seb. Cool as fuck that one. No more stairs but a door. It's easy to make decisions when there's only one option.

—We go through the door then, don't we? And make sure the dogs are with us.

I'm back in charge again. Open the door except I can't, it's locked.

—Stand back.

I give it a few kicks. Oh brilliant. That's my foot gone, definitely something's broke this time.

—What the fuck you doing standing back? Help us out here.

Seb karate kicks the door. It flies open. Result. Keep moving. Gotta keep moving. Can hear the sound of the security guards climbing the stairs behind us.

—What about a head count? Shona says.

—Eh?

—The dogs. Are they all here?

Jesus Christ. Paul starts laughing. He's borderline. Mental note to self. Never share a cupboard with Paul.

—We don't have time to count, I say.

But I scan them anyway, already half have run through the door. There's Norman. He's still with us.

—I'm pretty sure we've got them all. Let's go.

Through the door, fuck it's cold. Wait a second, where are we? An overhang and then I'm out in the open air. We're on the roof. The roof. It's quiet up here and the dogs are hushed by the stars. Have any of them ever been outside before? It floods back. No longer scared, just angry. None of these animals have ever breathed fresh air until now. A lab and a cage has been their world. The fuckers that did this are going to pay. Can't see Paul but Seb is staring over the city. What the hell is he pointing at?

—I think that's my house.

Either he's the coolest motherfucker on the planet or he's lost it.

—*The police are on their way. Don't move.*

A shout from below. Can't deal with Seb cracking up right now, just pretend he's all right.

—Seb, give us a hand, we gotta block the door.

The lock is broken but there's an old metal container, industrial bin maybe, lying not too far off. We grab it and wedge it against the door, should buy us some time.

—What are we going to do? Shona asks.

Uh-oh. I can sense something's happening to her, could be the beginnings of shock. Her face seems different.

—I don't know.

—Where's Paul? Seb says.

Yeah, where is Paul? I look over and see him begin to lower himself off the roof with nothing underneath.

—What you playing at? You're gonna kill yourself!

But he ignores me, his legs hanging.

—Seb, go and stop him from doing anything stupid.

Shona is at the lip of the roof, whispering to the puppy in her arms. The other dogs are waiting patiently at her feet. Norman rubs himself against my legs and I let him lick my hand as I walk to Shona and stand beside her.

—This has all gone wrong, hasn't it? she says.

—Yeah.

Her tone is freaking me out. I glance back but we're alone. Where the fuck are Paul and Seb?

　—It's nice up here. You get a really good view, she says.

Something bangs against the door. She doesn't even flinch. **BLAAAAM**. I jump but Shona's made of stone. It must be the facility's external alarm going off. The door bangs again. It won't be long now.

　—They're gonna put them back in the cages, aren't they? she says.

　—After we get out of prison we can try again. We'll bring collars next time.

She takes the puppy and shows me its neck, pulling back the fur. The skin underneath is punctured and bruised from countless injections. I'm not angry anymore just sad.

　—We can't let them go back to that.

Don't make me say it Shona, please don't, but she won't let me drop my eyes.

　—They'd be better off dead, I say.

Tell me go fuck myself, you can do it, you know you can. But she doesn't. Shona drops the puppy over the edge. And before I know it I'm flinging dogs to their deaths like there's no tomorrow, and there won't be, not after this.

　—*Open the door immediately.*

Cunts. They have driven me to this. Can't see through the tears that are streaming down my face but it doesn't matter cause the dogs aren't making any attempt to run, just sitting waiting for their turn. They trust us in the same way they trusted the doctors here. Norman actually jumps into my arms, Jesus Christ this is too much, but I'm doing this for your own good you gotta understand. And he's over the edge. I look about but there's only one left and Shona's taking care of it. God she looks weird. No tears, no emotion, nothing while I'm greetin' my eyes out. That's my girlfriend. The door cracks and when I look back to Shona it's done. None left. Our eyes meet but I have to look away. What the fuck, does this count as our first date? I can hear different voices on the other side of the door. They got reinforcements Danny. You're going down. And I can't help myself, like I've got Tourette's, and it must be because of what I've just done and I'm fucked up but I feel like the only peace and quiet I can get is if I can list my favourite prison films. At five. Clint Eastwood in *Escape From Alcatraz*. Danny don't do this. Four. Burt Reynolds *Mean Machine*. Shona needs you right now, comfort her. Three. Eric Bana *Chopper*. Who's gonna comfort me? Two. Paul Newman *Cool Hand Luke*. That should really be number one and I don't know if this even counts but the last has got to be –

—Danny! Seb screams at me.

—*Escape To Victory*. John Wark. Classic, I say.

—What?

—Nothing, you go first.

—You won't believe this but there's a fire escape on the floor below that we can drop onto. That's our way out!

The sound of breaking glass but coming from the inside. Or maybe it was the door. Yeah, the door. It's close to giving.

—Didn't you hear me? We can still make it. The dogs as well! He suddenly stops.

—Where are they?

I can't even shake my head. He gets on his hands and knees to look under a water tank, Jesus Christ, what does he think, we hid them?

—Where are the dogs, Danny?

Still can't answer.

    —Shona, what did you do to the dogs?

She doesn't answer him either, not even turning to look at him from the edge. The edge. She's on the fuckin' edge.

    —Stop going on about the fuckin' dogs Seb! Is that all you can talk about?

    —Eh? Sorry… Em. Danny, what's going on?

I grab her. She gives no resistance. Don't look at her face, can't take that right now. No time for thought only action. And the incredible truth is tonight could get worse if we stayed where we are.

    —Where's the fire escape then?

Seb finally gets the message.

    —This way.

I take her hand and we follow.

3

Last night. Forget about it. It doesn't matter. No Sir. It does not matter. What happened could have happened to anybody. That sort of thing probably goes on all the time, you just never hear about it. All part of the birth of a legend. Can't make an omelette without breaking some eggs. If you look at it in a certain way it could be funny. I should really laugh about it. Right this minute, have a good hearty laugh. The canteen's practically empty anyway, only Susan and she's too old, fifties, to mind people laughing out of context. Trauma in reverse. Laugh now, cry in five years time and then just act like it never happened. From where I'm sitting I can see the shop floor below, Ian and Tommy fannying about, Katie ignoring another customer, an old man, who's wanting to know where some piece of crap is to be found. At the front of the store a couple of young lads, trolley boys, trying to hide from Mark but he sees them and sends them out. At least I work inside and not in the car park where as well as the rain and the cold you've groups of wee dicks who take the piss. I couldn't handle that. 3pm. Another two hours to go before the shift is over. Before I get out of this hellhole. I've had some shit jobs but this has got to be the worst... Christ, I'll ask Mark if I can stay on. Anything's better than having time to think on my own. Too many thoughts.

That's a lie, too few. Just one on repeat if truth be told. Snap out of it Danny. You were going to laugh a minute ago. That's decided then. I bark a laugh. No, not a bark, please not a bark, the works canteen at Morrisons is not a good place to break down. Susan glances over, cow eyes, and laughs as well. Laugh and the world laughs with you.

—What the fuck you laughing at? I say.

She stops laughing, looks hurt, and consumes another mouthful of the reconstituted vomit that she's eating. Oh Christ. She could be your mum. Probably spent her whole life having cunts like you abuse her.

    —Susan, I'm sorry, I didn't mean it. Some bad things are going on up here (I tap my head), I'm sure you know what I'm talking about (don't give too much away). Mental problems. (Eh?)

She smiles and, oh fuck, I've let her in.

    —It's a'right son. I ken whit you're talkin' aboot.

I nod. We look at each other. First time I've ever properly taken her in. Slightly overweight, Deirdre type glasses, always took her expression as vacant but could be deep. Susan from the North. Maybe I've mistaken her. Maybe she really does know what I'm going through. Maybe she can help, a Scottish female version of Yoda.

    —She'll come back.

    —Eh?

    —The wee lassie yer pinin' over.

    —It's not a girl.

She laughs. What's her problem?

    —When a wee laddie's face is tripping him it's always cause o' a lassie.

—Not this time.

And laughs again. Who does she think she is, my mum?

—I'll let you into a secret, she says.

—It's ok.

—What no woman can resist.

In spite of myself I'm hooked.

—What's that then?

—I dinnae ken if I should tell you though. You might use it tae get lassie's pregnant.

My temperature is rising. She pushes her plate in my direction.

—Do you want the rest o' this?

The back end pastry of a sausage roll with the meat removed and a smear test of orange baked bean fluid.

—No thank you.

—I ken yer a veggie but aw the meat's been sucked oot.

Yes my dear, that is exactly how vegetarianism works.

—Just the information please.

Suddenly this is the most important thing in the world. I need to know.

—What's the secret no woman can resist? I say.

She leans towards me and glances at the door. We are a conspiracy. This better be good.

—Chocolates.

The enormity of her answer and everything it means overwhelms me. What about honesty, truth and understanding? What about respect and consideration? What about oral clitoral stimulation that can take a woman to places men can only dream about?

—Ye ken, like those mini-Celebrations.

Somebody has got to sort her out. For her own good. I'd be doing her a favour.

—Or flowers.

—What?

—Flowers.

Did she just fucking wink at me? Here it comes. Sorry Susan but you need to hear the truth. I am not responsible for what I'm going to say. Your existence is about to be analysed and destroyed piece by piece. Her eyes drop to the plastic table and then shyly back to mine. Oh no, she's going to share.

—Naebody's ever given me flowers. And that's aw I ever wanted, ye ken, just somebody to give me flowers for myself. I got flowers given to me at my ma's funeral but it wisnae the same. Wisnae romantic.

But I can't speak, can't sort her out, because I'm crying. I bend down and have a coughing fit in a pathetic attempt to hide the sobs.

—Ah!

She hits me on the back. She can't really think I'm coughing? Or maybe she realises that the best way to deal with this situation is to play along? She hits me again. No, she genuinely thinks I'm coughing and it makes me laugh. I wipe my face. I feel better.

—Thanks Susan.

I smile at her and she smiles back. The door opens and Mark pokes his head in. Perhaps I don't need to ask for an extra shift tonight. I'll go home and phone Shona again. Maybe she'll pick up this time. She could probably do with someone to talk to. She's not as strong as I am.

—Danny, Mark says.

—Yeah.

—You're a trolley boy. Get a bib.

4

Shona's not here yet but she said she'd come. Sounded a bit down on the phone when I eventually got through to her and it didn't seem right to talk about us. *Us.* Do that today. It's Saturday, and tonight is Saturday night, perfect time for a date. She did say yes, didn't she? At least I'm out, on the street, doing something. Still having problems sleeping. That's ok, to be expected, can handle it. Ahead, partially hiding us from the public view, some guys with a Revolutionary Socialist Worker stall handing out leaflets but mostly just looking kinda threatening, and to the left the environmentalist hippie. Usually there's a few of them but he's on his own today. Some people passing by but not paying attention. Can't tell what Seb's feeling, his scarf over his face. No such problem with Paul, he looks bored. Been here an hour and hardly any action. No money, no signatures, nobody giving a fuck.

   —This is embarrassing. We always arrive late and get the
   shit spot. Next time we arrive at 8am, got that? I say.
Seb nods but Paul isn't paying attention, his eyes on the street.

   —We were in the papers again yesterday, Seb says.
Not sure if I want to know but have to ask.

—What'd they say?

—'Medical research staff fail to save victims of animal cruelty,'.

And stretches his arms out like a billboard.

—That was the banner headline. Page three, roughly two hundred word article –

—Who cares about the number of fucking words! That's unbelievable. They're making us out as the bad guys? The media in this country is a joke.

—Be fair. You and Shona did fling them off the roof, Paul says.

I look at him, Jesus Christ, the bastard's smirking.

—Fuck off. And don't you dare say that when Shona is about. She's bound to be upset an' that'll just make it worse.

He shrugs and turns away, a smile on his lips.

—I suppose there is one positive we can take out of it, Seb says.

—This better be good man, I'm in a bit of a state myself.

—Well, the police aren't looking for animal lovers like us, they think that only deranged *animal haters* could have killed twenty five dogs by tossing them off a roof.

I stare at Seb. This guy is a mystery. Lives in a commune, could explain a lot.

—Don't say that to Shona either, I say.

—What can we say to her? Paul says.

Lack of sleep must be playing with my head because I'm getting the feeling that Paul is enjoying this.

—Don't say anything man. Y'know, you shouldn't have said anything to me either. I've not been eating the cheese but I've been having the fuckin' nightmares.

—… Sorry, Seb says.

And I can tell he means it, he even semi-touches my arm. Good lad Seb. Always know I can trust him. He looks up to me, like a cool older brother maybe.

—Give me a collecting can, Paul says.

He takes it and walks past the socialists into the main stream of people. Seb takes out a flyer from his pocket.

—You seen this Danny? The Circus is coming to town next month –

—Put that fucking thing away Seb! I mean it. I can't handle the Circus, not today.

We stand in silence for a few seconds but Seb is too full of life to keep quiet for long.

—Any luck so far? Seb says to the hippie next to us.

He's about fifty, goatee beard, long hair but balding at the same time. He's done even worse than us, no one's been near his stall all morning, and I only notice it for the first time now, but there is nothing to show what he's trying to push. No literature, no signs, no petitions. Hmmm.

—It's where we are, know what I mean?

He points to the stall in front of us.

—It's funny how it's the reds that always take the best spots.

Spider sense is tingling.

—They care as much about the earth as the capitalists do. What's the point of giving the means of production to the proletariat if at the same time you've killed all the trees? he says.

—Or all the animals, Seb says.

The hippie nods. I slightly nudge Seb in the ribs to get him to leave it. The hippie cups his hands around his mouth and gives it all he's got.

—Commie Bastards!

A few hefty looking blokes turn round and give us dirty looks. The hippie eyeballs them aggressively while I smile and shake my head, trying to get the message across that he's nothing to do with us. But that's it for now. They get back to what they're doing. The hippie laughs.

—Where are the others? Usually there's quite a few of you. Seb says.

—Yeah. We split. Ideological differences. I'm on my own now. Uh-oh.

—What do you think of this? he says.

The hippie rummages in a rucksack at his feet and pulls out a t-shirt with the slogan 'Fucking Tree Hugger And Proud' printed on it.

—… That's quite impressive, I say.

I try to focus on the street but out of the corner of my eye I see him put the t-shirt on a stick and start waving it above his head. Next week we *need* to get here earlier. I watch Paul chatting to two 16 year-old lassies. They shriek with laughter and head off. What did he say to them? I start to move in his direction but stop. A slight female figure dressed totally in black and wearing a balaclava is heading towards us. She passes Paul without a glance and makes her way to the stall, stopping without saying a word a foot or so from me.

—Shona, is that you?

She nods. A balaclava. This is not good.

—Danny, can we all dress like that? She looks brilliant! Seb says.

Seb is so impressed he's practically bouncing up and down. Time to get him out of here. I thrust some leaflets in his hands.

—Go and help Paul.

Seb takes them but lingers for a second before going, marvelling at Shona's new look. I shuffle towards her. She crosses her arms. I shuffle back. Ok, best just to dive straight in.

—How you feeling about last week?

She doesn't answer.

—Don't be worried if you've had trouble sleeping or anything... Terrible nightmares. Cold sweats. Not even cold sweats, just sweats –

—I feel fine, she says. –Don't ask again.

That'll be that then. Best leave it there for now. No point rushing things. There's some movement in the stall in front of us but I ignore it. Come on Danny, there's obviously something you can say that would totally sort everything out. Fuck it, I'll ask her if she wants a chewing gum, wait a second, could be perceived as an insult, she might think I'm accusing her of having bad breath?

—Can I have a word, mate?

It's one of the guys calling over from the Revolutionary Socialist Workers stall. Big bastard and he doesn't look happy, politically correct but with steel toecaps. There's a fair squad of them and they're all staring at us. I saunter over and put on a front. No point letting them know the truth.

—We got a problem, he says.

—Yeah?

—It's urban terrorist girl over there, he says.

He points at Shona. I follow the direction of his finger. I have to agree with him. The balaclava was a mistake. Makes me realise how much I like her face, her hair... Enough Danny, this isn't the time to think about her hair.

—What about her?

—She's gonna put people off. The public will think that
we're collecting for terrorist organisations, which is no
fuckin' good. That is not the message we want to send out.
I'm still looking at her and hearing his words and who the fuck
does this guy think he is?

—Give her a break eh? She's been through a lot recently.

—I'm really sorry about that but it's got sod all to do with
us. Tell her to take the balaclava off or leave.

—This is a free country pal –

He prods me in the shoulder and it hurts but at least I don't
show it. He could probably kick my head in on his own never
mind the mates he's got backing him up.

—Take care of it or we will, he says.

On the bright side he obviously recognises the fact that I'm the
leader and the one he has to talk to about any executive decisions. I return. Seb's back beside Shona.

—What was that about? he says.

—They want Shona to take the balaclava off. They think its
sending out the wrong signals.

She nods ever so slightly.

—They're total arseholes but... I suppose you might as well,
I mean –

Where the hell's she going? Shona's past me before I can react
and squaring up to the guy I was just talking to. I run and get in
between them.

—You got a problem with what I'm wearing? she says.

—Come on, we can sort this out without any trouble, I say.

They ignore me. The hippie's appeared, now wearing his 'Fucking
Tree Hugger And Proud' top.

—Get rid of the fuckin' balaclava, the socialist says.
The hippie sticks his chin out.

—She'll take it off when you stop being such a cunting shit-face.
We don't need this.

—This man does not represent us –
But the rest of what I'm saying is lost as Shona overturns their stall sending it crashing to the ground and the leaflets flying. The guy grabs her arm but I punch him in the face and he lets her go. There's too many of them and now I'm the one grabbing Shona's arm and pulling her away. It's time to run and after a second she realises this as well and we're off before the others can properly react. Pass Paul and he takes one look and joins us. We turn a corner and there's no sign of any pursuit. I slow to a walk. Have spent too much time getting chased recently, it's embarrassing.

—Who wants to go for a drink? I say.

The pub is full of young people, mostly students, having a good time. But I can spot four who don't seem to be in such high spirits. Perhaps it was my fault, only buying half pints was probably a mistake, but I'm skint and nobody else was offering. Shona still has the balaclava on. Time to inject some energy.

—The bulls of Pamplona, I say.
And lift my glass. The others half-heartedly raise their half pints but don't drink.

—Shona. Please. Could you take the balaclava off?
For a second I think she's gonna tell me to go fuck myself but then in one movement pulls it from her head. Her hair's been shaved off and her face is flushed red. Right Danny, you're her boyfriend, it's your job to be supportive.

—I really like what you've done with your hair, I say.
Paul is staring with his mouth open and I try to get him to act
cool with a flash of my eyes but he's not having any of it.

    —Do you realise how red your face is? That can't be healthy.
    Maybe you should think about a beret instead? he says.

    —I'll lose the balaclava when the war is over. Not before,
    Shona says.

Nobody speaks. I see a couple, early 20s, my age, at the bar
having a really good laugh. Glowing in that way that they know
they're in love and going to have sex at some point in the near
future. Have to fight the temptation to wish them cancer.

    —Why don't we go out tonight? Let our hair down, I say.
But there's no response, apart from Paul who sniggers and
glances at Shona. Fuck, I didn't mean to say that.

    —What we got planned for next week? Seb says.
He saved me there. Good lad. Now then, this is where I get my
reputation back. Right some wrongs. I've put a lot of thought
into this and props are always impressive. I lean across the table
and lower my voice.

    —Next week we're on active duty. We can either join up
    with the hunt saboteurs or –

    —Aren't fox hunts illegal now? Paul says.

    —They're supposed to be but that doesn't stop them, Seb says.

    —Excuse me, I wasn't finished, I say. —We can go along to
    the hunt or we can do *something else.*

That got their attention, well Shona's and Seb's anyway. Paul's
staring at a girl who's wearing a short skirt. He's practically
drooling. Fear suddenly invades, is this the way I look when I
check women out? That terrible moment on the bus when I got
caught...

—We can join up with the hunt saboteurs or what? Seb says.

I pull out a set of handcuffs and slam them onto the table.

—Fuckin' McDonalds man! I got handcuffs without keys. Let's see what they think about that!

Seb and Shona don't say anything.

—Y'know, attach ourselves to the radiators. Bring it down from the inside.

It sounded a lot better in my head.

—Where d'you get those handcuffs? Paul says.

And lifts them from the table.

—It doesn't matter, I say.

He notices something on the handcuffs and laughs.

—These are from Ann Summers!

Oh fuck.

—No they're not, I say.

—Aye they are, it says so on them.

—The point isn't where I got them the point is what we're gonna do with them.

But Paul isn't giving up.

—I saw these advertised in the window. You got the handcuffs free if you spent more than twenty quid. So what else did you buy?

And apart from anything else that's a lie. That is a fucking lie.

—Paul you're a cunt and I'm only gonna say this once. I didn't get them from Ann Summers but you can think what you want cause I really couldn't give a toss.

I look at Seb and Shona, ignoring him. Back me up here, please.

—So what's it to be? The hunt or McDonalds? I say.

—The hunt, Shona says.

Seb nods. Fair enough. Jesus though, I got feelings too. I mean, at least I'm trying.

—I know some people. They might come to the hunt as well, Shona says.

Whoa there cowboy.

—Who?

—You've not met them. They're into serious action.

—Yeah? So am I.

She doesn't answer and I don't have the heart to push it. The young couple have met another young couple and they appear to be playing a drinking game. Bastards.

—That's next week's sorted then, I say. —What about tonight? How about a pub crawl?

—I'm off, Paul says, –I have a date.

He waits, expecting us to ask who with, but I'm not gonna and Seb and Shona don't bother either.

—Fine, he says.

He gets up and I watch him go. For a split second it looks like he might go into the ladies' toilet but obviously thinks better of it and heads out onto the street. He's the one with the problems, not me. Shona is staring out of the window and Seb is sipping his cider. That's what living on a commune does for you, I suppose. He's probably been drinking that piss since birth. He's always clean though, I'll give him that. Should really visit him sometime. I let out a little whistle.

—I'm not saying we should do everything together but the occasional social gathering might be good for morale. We could treat it like a works night out or something? I say.

Seb downs his cider and gets to his feet.

—Sorry Danny but I've got to go. See you later Shona. Love the new look.

—See ya Seb.

And he's away. We're alone. Saturday night, well afternoon, and I'm in the pub with her. Does this count as a date? I hope not, because if it is it's a disaster. Seconds turn into a minute of silence. We're one of those couples that you see sitting in restaurants not talking. Together but so obviously not. Difference is they're usually in their fifties. That's quick work Danny, well done, you've cut out all the fun and experimental sex and gone straight to the dead end. Fuck up Danny. You can save this. Her hands are on the table, tempting me. I place one of mine a few centimetres away but that's as far as I dare.

—To be honest, I'm kinda glad that Paul and Seb didn't want to come out tonight, I say.

—I don't want to go out either.

I should have seen that one coming. My cheeks begin to prickle and I suddenly see the benefit of wearing a balaclava, you could cry constantly and no one would notice.

—Last week –

—I don't want to talk about last week, she says.

I nod. Leave it Danny, leave it. But I can't.

—It's just, remember when we were hiding in the cupboard? There was talk of like… y'know, the pictures or something?

I shouldn't speak anymore and am humiliating myself but it all comes flooding out.

—I mean, are we going out? You turn up dressed like you are, start a fight with those arseholes, shave your hair off, don't get me wrong I like it, but I liked your other hair as well. Last week was a fuckin' nightmare but –

She looks me directly in the eyes and it's enough to shut me up.

—I am not the same person I was last week. Forget everything you thought you knew about me. You're lucky I'm letting you call me Shona.

So this isn't a date then. You need to be going out to have a date, even a disastrous one.

—What you doing for the rest of the day? I say.

But I'm not really here. The pub's getting busier, more couples. What is this bar anyway? A fucking knocking shop?

—Going home. Staying in.

—That could be good, a bit of quiet time, contemplation. Get your head sorted.

—I'm going to spend the evening hitting a piece of wood, she says.

That brings me back. I look at her hands on the table. Holy shit, the knuckles are all cut and bruised. But as soon as I've seen them and she sees me seeing them she takes them from the table. Oh God Shona, I'm sorry, I'm so sorry.

—What about you? she says.

I try to smile but trying isn't the same as doing.

—Don't worry about me. I got big plans.

She gets up.

—I'll phone you about next week. The hunt. I'm looking forward to it.

She slips out of the door. Check the time. 4pm. I've still got half my half pint left and there's no way I'm going to just leave it. I am an adult. I can sit and have a drink on my own in a pub without feeling self-conscious. It's a sign of maturity. They do this all the time in Paris. Finish my quarter pint in about a minute and that was me taking it slow. Shona hardly touched hers and it stares at me from across the table. A practically full half pint that her lips have graced. Lean over and take it. Raise it to my mouth. This is romantic. This is a kiss. Pity it's warm and flat but I savour it anyway. Stick my tongue out to taste the glass in case there's still some of her on it but it just tastes like glass. Oh shit, I've spilled most of it down my top. What was I thinking sticking my tongue in it for fucksake? Down the rest. Paul left some dregs and they're next. A couple in the table beside me get up and go and there's a good measure of vodka tonic left in the girl's glass. Pretend to stretch and use that as cover to pick it up and suck it down before the table's taken by another happy fucking couple. Oh yeah, this is exactly like the Parisian café culture.

   —Anyone sitting here?

A group of three young guys. The one that spoke is the only normal looking one, the other two got a Goth little and large thing going on.

   —Yeah. Sorry, I say.

But they stay standing beside me anyway as there are no other tables free. Shit. Why didn't I just let them have the table? Now I can't without them knowing I was lying about the seats being taken. Not that it matters but still. Everything matters. The small Goth points at a couple of girls at the other end of the bar, his hand brushing against the side of my head which we both pretend didn't happen.

   —What about them? he says.

   —Naw, they're dogs, the big Goth answers.

This coming from a guy whose face looks like a dog shit sprinkled with acid. Always made me laugh. People, well men, talking about what they want in the opposite sex. The colour of hair,

RAYMOND FRIEL

eyes, body type. The exact conditions that will make up their future partner. As if it's got anything to do with them. The vast majority of men will marry the first woman that shows them any interest whatsoever and be eternally grateful for it.

—I know but what if they're dirty? the wee one says.

—What if they are?

The normal one speaks and they defer. He is the voice of authority here, presumably because he's the only one who wouldn't get work in a freak show.

—Question, he says –what's more important, looks or how dirty the girl is?

Fucking hell. That's all I need, forced eavesdropping on a misogynist conversation. And anyway, it's dirty every time. I take out my phone and pretend I'm answering a call.

—What? You can't make it? I say. –Thanks a lot.

That sounded pathetic even to me so God knows how it sounded to them. They can have my table, I'm outta here.

Another pub. At the bar. Half sitting on a stool with one leg propping me up. This drinking on your own business isn't so bad. Once you're drunk it really doesn't seem an issue, why did I ever think it was? Better than going home anyway. Just smiling at folk as they pass me by. Who could have a problem with that?

—Hey.

Oh shit. The two thirty-something women I've been intermittently staring at are now at my side. I lower my head and don't say anything.

—I'm talking to you.

An English accent. The one speaking, short black hair and big brown eyes, would be out of my league even if I was in top form, and let's face it, it's been a while, pokes me in the shoulder. Oh my God I'm about to get a kicking,

 —Me? I say.

 —Yeah you. You've been staring at us haven't you?

 —No I haven't.

 —Yes you have.

 —No I haven't.

 —Yes you have.

Right, best just to come clean and apologise. Could offer them money? No Danny, that'll just make it worse.

 —I'm sorry, I say. –I'd better go.

But I've got a fair bit of my drink left and I'm not walking out on that so as I stand I gulp it down.

 —Don't go, she says. –Just, if you like what you see fancy
 coming back to our hotel with us to... y'know?

Spit the last mouthful of lager over myself. Did I just hear that? And now they're both smiling suggestively, no not suggestively, twitchily, which is more intimidating than the poke on the shoulder.

 —Y'know? I say.

 —Y'know, the other one says.

I don't know. I really really don't know. She's got long auburn hair, a bit like Shona's. What Shona's used to be like. She licks her lips, her tongue feeling the top of her gums. They're both doing it. Are they on something?

 —To have sex, she says.

I laugh. And so do they, but not in a bad way. They've got a sense of humour.

 —Yeah I'd love to. That's what I was thinking when I was
 staring at you, I say.

—Get your coat then, you've pulled, the black haired one says.

I laugh again but this time they don't join in, already heading towards the exit. They turn round.

—What you waiting for? the long haired one says.

—Em, are you serious?

—Yeah. Why wouldn't we be?

Oh God this *is* going to end in a kicking. I bet there's a giant skinhead called Psycho Ralph waiting for me in their room with an axe. And if by some incredible stroke of fortune there isn't, the best I can hope for is that this is a cruel practical joke for a hidden camera show and they're a pair Jeremy Beadles with tits. I shake my head. I might be drunk but I'm not a complete clown. No Danny, not a clown, never a clown.

—This isn't right is it? I say —It's a set up.

They look at each other and then back at me.

—Is it so hard to believe that both of us want to have sex with you? the black haired woman says.

—Yeah, that's pretty much it.

—Why?

Even if they are on drugs it doesn't give them the right to fuck with my head. I was smiling a minute ago and now all I feel is tightness in my gut. Not for you. That's what this is. Those two might as well be holding a big fucking sign with NOT FOR YOU written on it. And that doesn't just go for threesomes, you can add to the list getting a job you actually like, snowboarding in the Alps, winning a fight, having friends that won't backstab you, owning an Xbox which doesn't get the Red Ring Of Death. NOT FOR YOU. Designer shops and safaris. NOT FOR YOU. Basically anything that is good or brilliant or unexpectedly amazing you can replace with a giant billboard with twenty foot letters like the ones on the hill overlooking Hollywood. NOT FOR YOU. And underneath it, in slightly smaller letters but still ten feet or something – FUCK OFF. And just underneath *them*, in one foot letters, the small print: *What were you even thinking, that you could ever have any of this?* And she's asking me why it's so hard to believe that they want to have sex with me?

    —I'll tell you why, I say. –Cause on the one hand there's you asking me to go back to your hotel for a threesome and on the other hand there is fucking reality.

Can't help it, getting angry. I didn't need this.

    —Fucking reality? the black haired one says.

    —Fucking reality. Stuff like this doesn't happen to guys like me so you can tell Psycho Ralph to put his chopper away.

    —Who's Psycho Ralph –

I cut her off.

    —Or you're blokes. You're blokes with huge cocks and if I go back with you you'll turn me into a woman.

The auburn haired woman takes my hand and places it on her chest.

    —Okay… So you're not blokes then, I say.

She lets go of my hand and it falls limply to my side. They walk out the door. A bullet dodged.

Another pub. Another seat at the bar. Vespbar opposite the Horseshoe. Have calmed down. That's it, no more smiling (or staring) at anyone. Now understand why the old guys you see in pubs never make eye contact with anyone. Should go home but still can't, at least this is taking my mind off things. Shona and Norman. Dead dogs. Stop right there. Think of something else. Happy thoughts. Danny, here's the thing, what if those girls had been genuine? Who you trying to kid, even then it would still have been a disaster. I know it's supposedly the number one fantasy for men, two women, actually that's not true. It's the second most popular fantasy. The first is the zombie holocaust. Or to be precise, being the hero in a zombie holocaust/sinking ship/or some other staple disaster film scenario. God knows the amount of hours I must have spent when I was a kid daydreaming about some situation where I was the hero. In most of them I would end up dying to save the planet, a martyr complex which I don't want to analyse too much. Pathetic, yes, but according to this survey all men do it, and anyway, it's actually life affirming. Better to fantasise about saving lives than ending them. Or ending them with good intentions. Get back to the threesome Danny. Concentrate. Let's pretend they weren't trying to mug you (which they definitely were). You go back to their hotel room. Have a drink. A few more laughs. Get naked. It's around here that the problems would start.

—So... , I'd say.

—So what? they'd answer.

—So, em, I'm probably better off just watching for a bit.

—If you're only going to watch then what's the point of you being here?

—Don't be like that –

—Don't be like what?

Bastards would probably gang up on me. Better off being mugged. Fuck, getting angry again, don't feel drunk but almost slipped off the stool there thinking about the threesome. Threesome, that's a laugh, they should just call it what it is, a despair sandwich.

—You looking for a good time? a young studenty guy says to me.

What sort of vibe am I giving out today?

—Comedy show about to start, he says. –It's free.

I follow him downstairs and through a door. Oh fuck what have I done? I'm the only person here and he practically drags me by the hand to a seat at the front before jumping onto what counts as the stage.

—Thank you all for coming, he says.

—Mate, I need to go, I say.

—Please don't go, he says. –Tons more will be here soon.

—I have to.

—Just wait for the first gag. Give me that.

He flashes me a desperate smile. This is his dream, just go along with it Danny. Consider it charity work.

—Thanks, he says. –Have you heard about near-death experiences?

And nods at me wanting a response.

—Em, yeah, I've heard about near-death experiences, I say.

—Great! You'll love this then. So near death-experiences, bright lights and pearly gates and everything. Now, what they don't tell you is that ten per cent of all near-death experiences don't end up so great. Ten per cent of all near death-experiences aren't brief visits to heaven but are journeys to hell!

—Fuck off, I say.

—Are you heckling me? he says. –Because if you are I've prepared a putdown.

—No, I mean, that's not true is it? I say.

—Straight up. Folk who've had one of these bad near-death experiences think God has abandoned them and they are damned for eternity. Apparently it's a lot higher than ten per cent in failed suicide attempts.

This is the most terrifying thing I have ever heard.

—Which brings me to the funny bit, he says. —So imagine you've tried to kill yourself and your stomach is being pumped but you're in hell and Satan appears –

I'm going to be sick and run for the door.

—You could have waited for the punchline! he calls after me. But I'm up the stairs and outside just as the vomit comes shooting from my mouth and splashes onto the pavement. People passing by but I am utterly alone. That fucking comedian. I need someone to talk to. Take out my phone and am calling Shona before I know it. It rings and rings and rings.

—Leave a message after the tone.

I put the phone away. There is no one else. Then I see Paul just ahead about to go into a club at the end of the street. Even Paul's better than nothing.

—Paul!

He's already inside and I go after him. The glow of red neon. Can't see him. Bouncer at the door, oh fuck, I'm wrecked and stink of sick there's no way he's letting me in.

—Tenner, he says.

So surprised that he's not telling me to piss off that I'm paying him and get inside before it registers. Feeling dizzy and worried I'm gonna spew again so keep my head down and go straight to the bar. Don't make eye contact but the guy serving comes over anyway.

—What do you want?

—Water.

—Still or sparkling? he says.

—... Tap.

He pauses like he's not gonna serve me.

—Pint of lager, the cheapest, I say.

I hand him the last of my money and he goes to get it. I take some deep breaths and by the time the barman is back with the drink I don't feel like throwing up. A stunning girl appears at my side and I'm praying she's not gonna notice the smell when she practically rubs herself against me.

—Do you want a dance?

What the hell is going on? First the threesome and now this?

—I'd love to but I'm too drunk to dance, I say.

—Not you, me.

Raise my head and focus on my surroundings. Oh for fuckssake. I'm in a pole dancing club. Not very busy and only a couple of girls dancing at the far end which is why I didn't notice when I came in. Paul you bastard.

—Yeah, of course. Sorry, maybe later.

She turns and floats away. I scan the room but can't see any sign of him. Too ashamed to look at the girls and check out the punters instead. As expected a pretty dire bunch, though not quite in the obvious dirty mac stinking of pish way. Apart from me. A few guys in their thirties who look like they've got money. A bored dancer in a blue bikini is gyrating in front of the only other person here who looks almost as drunk as I am. He stands up and thrusts a ten-pound note into her top, trying – but failing – to grope her breasts as she sways away from him.

—Hey! I want change, he says.

And points towards the fruit machine next to the bar.

—For the puggy. You keep a fiver and give me the rest in coins, yeah?

But she ignores him and slides around the pole. Zoom in on a guy in his sixties who looks vaguely like my old physics teacher at a table watching a girl dressed as a dominatrix. He takes a drink and I see the glint of a wedding ring. Can't help but picture the path he's taken to get to this place. Him and his wife in the bedroom on a Saturday night.

—It's just role play, that's all, he says. —Nothing to be frightened of. It's good for married couples like us to keep things interesting.

—I don't think I'd be very good at it, she says.

—Look, it's very simple, I'm a slave, you're my mistress. I get turned on by being abused so just let rip.

She shakes her head. It doesn't feel right.

—Here, I'll start you off, you're filth, call me filth, he says.

—… You're filth? she says quietly.

—That's it! We're on our way!

—You're a toilet?

—I'm a toilet! I *am* a toilet! Don't say it as a question though, remember you're in charge.

Suddenly the mood changes. She sees him as he truly is.

—You deserve to be pee'd on. You're nothing, worthless, your tongue should lick boots all day, she says.

—This is lovely stuff –

—And you're a wanker. A complete and utter tosser.

—Eh?

But there's no stopping her now.

—My mother was right, I'd have been better off marrying the speaking clock, at least then I'd be able to get the time, unlike you who refuses to wear the watch I bought you for Christmas.

—Em, I'm not really enjoying this anymore, he says.

—I'm sorry darling, I though this is what you wanted?

—Sort of but can we keep it to filth and toilets?

—As you wish. Get on your knees slave.

He drops to the floor and looks up at her expectantly.

—You are a terrible –

This is it, his fantasy becomes reality.

—You are a terrible –

Everything he ever dreamed about.

—You are a terrible father.

And so he ends up in a pole dancing club staring at something he can never have. It's the *Fifty Shades of Grey* phenomenon. A lot of men bought the book for their wives to spice things up but then the women got really into it and most of the guys regretted buying them the book in the first place. Be careful what you wish for. Another girl way beyond my pay grade approaches and I run away from her and hide at a table in an alcove. There's almost a whole unfinished drink which goes down pretty quick and takes the taste of sick from my mouth. Still got the pint I bought from the bar which I can nurse. A big crowd of guys enter, looks like a stag night from the level of drunkenness and forced high spirits. There are suddenly a lot more girls around, sensing the chance to make some money and the stag party don't disappoint, their faces greasy with lust. Directly in front of me, one of them is talking to a girl in the highest heels I've ever seen. She laughs at something he whispers in her ear as she takes a twenty pound note off him.

—I heard your father was a thief, he says.

—What? she says.

—I heard your father was a thief, he says again.

She doesn't look happy, the fake smile gone. He must have touched a nerve.

—Who told you that? she says.

—No, I heard your father was a thief because –

—So what if my dad's in jail? What sort of prick are you?

And then she's signalling to a bouncer and the guy is practically lifted off his feet and carried to the door.

—Because he stole the stars and put them in your eyes, he shouts.

But she's not listening and the bouncer doesn't care. His pals laugh and not one of them goes after him. So busy watching this I'd forgotten why I came here in the first place. Paul. And then I see him coming out of a door behind the stage. There's something strange about the way he's moving, agitated, and he's glancing behind him as if he's worried about being chased. He passes my table without seeing me, is he crying? I'm about to call out but before I can he jumps onto a small raised platform with a free pole in front of the stag party.

—Is this what you want? he shouts –Is this what you want? He tries to pull his top off but it gets tangled over his head and there's already a couple of bouncers heading his way and after seeing what they did to the last guy fuck knows what they're going to do to him. I get up and push my way through the stags and grab his hand.

—Paul, c'mon.

—Danny? What you doing here?

—Same as you, leaving.

I drag him off the stage and the bouncers are closing in but we make it down the stairs and onto the street. Doesn't look like they're coming after us. Paul stops to put his t-shirt back on. It's getting busy but we must seem pretty mental even for Glasgow on a Saturday night and nobody looks our way.

—What the fuck was that about? I say.

—Nothing, he says.

—Why did you go on the pole?

—I was trying to fund my way through university.

—Ha ha, very funny. Why did you do it really?

He looks back to the entrance to the club and wipes his nose with his hand.

—... They have my wee sister, he says.

—Who does?

—They do. The strip club. They've kidnapped her.

—They've kidnapped her?

—Yeah.

Something's not right here.

—Well phone the police then.

—It's not as simple as that... She's too good to be working there.

Oh I get it. Protective big brother syndrome. I don't have a sister but I can understand where he's coming from. I put my hand on his shoulder. He is an animal in need.

—I hear you but it's a free country.

—That's rich coming from you. You're always going on about how we live in a police state.

He's got me there. One of the bouncers from the club appears and points at us from across the road.

—Come here again and we'll call the police.

—Give him a break, he just wants to talk to his sister, I say.

—Who? the bouncer says.

—His sister –

The bouncer starts to laugh and suddenly Paul is pulling me away.

—Danny, we'd better go, we don't want to be lifted.

—What about your wee sister?

—Fuck her.

I let myself be led and then we're on Union Street. So many drunk people, thank God I'm drunk too or they'd be giving me a panic attack.

—She's not really your sister is she? I say.

—No.

—You're stalking one of the dancers aren't you?

—I'm not fucking stalking her! he shouts. –It's just, last week you wouldn't believe how well we were getting on and then tonight it's like I don't exist.

—You were paying her for fuckssake!

—It wasn't like that –

—But you were paying her weren't you?

—… The whole night.

—Christ that must have set you back, I say.

—Dances are half price Tuesday to Thursday –

—The point is this Paul, you were paying her and let me guess, you didn't have much money on you tonight?

He shakes his head.

—I love her Danny, he says. –Nicola. Her name's Nicola. You know what it's like.

Please don't tell me what I have for Shona is the same as this. We're crossing Sauchiehall Street, towards St Enoch's. Various groups of lads who're looking for trouble but as long as we walk quickly we're alright.

—Do you believe in love at first sight? he says.

—Not in a strip club.

—Why not?

—Cause she got one of the bouncers to threaten you with the police that's why not!

—I don't mean for her I mean for me?

I don't say anything. I suppose it could be romantic, well not romantic exactly, more like something you'd see in an American rom-com with Ashton Kutcher in the lead. As in shite.

—Yeah, okay. Love's love I suppose, I say.

—She's the one, you know, the one for me, he says.

Crossing St Enoch's now, always hated this part of town, was almost mugged at a cash machine here once.

—Where we going by the way? I say.

—There's another pole dancing club just down from the old Fury Murrys –

—You have got to be kidding.

That's it for me. Home, no matter how bad that is, is better than being with Paul.

—I'm off, I say.

Paul stops.

—You're right, he says –Forget the strip club, there's no deals on tonight anyway. I got some beers at my place?

Paul's flat. Shouldn't be here. If I'm always slightly embarrassed about being a bit of a slob he has obviously moved well beyond that. He tosses some clothes onto the ground to make space for me on the sofa. Big TV in the corner of the room, DVDs stacked beside it, even some old VHS tapes. He sees where I'm looking and picks up a DVD box set.

—You ever heard of this? *Manimal*. It was on back in the day.

—No, I say.

—It's weird isn't it? he says. —We all say back in the day now, but we never said back in the day, back in the day.

—Good point, well made, I say.

—So *Manimal*, he says, —it's about a guy that can turn into animals to solve crimes. Hence the name, *Manimal*. Total crap to be honest, the only good thing about it was the moment at the end of every episode when an exotic animal would appear, like an elephant or giraffe or a crocodile, and there would be a split second when Brooke, the woman on the cover, thought it was Jonathan. Then he would appear in human form and they would both laugh about it. One time she even started a conversation with a fly thinking it was him, the stupid cow.

He goes to the kitchen to get the beers and I take a look at his DVDs. Mostly TV shows, some stuff I've never heard of like *Matt Houston*, cop programmes, *The Bill*, *Dexter*, *Miami Vice*, *CSI*, *Without A Trace*, even the TV pilot for *Cagney and Lacey*. Read the back, Cagney and Lacey go undercover as prostitutes. Look at the next, *Dempsey and Makepeace*, and scan the synopsis. Makepeace goes undercover as a prostitute… Quick glance at all the rest, oh for fuckssake, each one is an episode where the female cop goes undercover as a prostitute, a helluva lot of *Miami Vice* here, they must have had whole seasons based around this concept. There's even an episode of *Smallville* where Lois is at it too. Paul returns with two small bottles of Biere Deluxe, Asda's own brand, and hands me one.

—Cheers, I say.

But don't drink. I put it in my pocket and get the fuck out of there.

5

Morrisons carpark, half full. This isn't so bad. At least I'm out in the fresh air and it's not raining. Shame about the bib but being a trolley boy (*man*, I am 22 after all) is not the end of the world. Gives me a bit more time to think about things. Not things, let's leave things as they are. Spent too much time going over *things*. Last week couldn't sleep, this week slept too much. Or at least been in bed too much, all day Sunday in a state of semi-consciousness. Never understood that masturbating constantly could be a sign of depression (it doesn't make sense, it just doesn't) but now not so sure. Peaks and troughs but the peaks getting smaller as the troughs get deeper until any momentary high flatlines around the eighth wank and the fantasy required to go again produces only self-disgust. I should never have done it in the bath, it came out all stringy and then clung to me like a slime nighty and I had to have a shower immediately afterwards to get clean. Cumming when not even fully erect can only lead to madness. The masturbation stops now. Got the hunt to look forward to. Even the score a bit. What's it at now anyway? Let's see, I became a vegetarian when I was seven, after the Circus and the incident with the clown. Ok, probably had some sort of meat once a day for about five years before then, so that's, what? One thousand eight hundred and seventy five in the negative column. One thousand eight hundred and seventy five animals killed because of me. Add to that the twenty five dogs I flung off the roof. That's a cool nineteen hundred. Woah. Shit. Don't linger Danny, look at the positives. Positives, Samson (Jack Russell), saved from the cat and dog home. Samson, legendary, they'll still be talking about him after I'm long gone. Probably shouldn't have done that speech at school about him being my best friend, at seventeen it's no surprise I got pelters for it. Asking for trouble... School. The fact that I don't keep in touch with anybody I knew then is that a bad thing? And even though I wasn't bullied does not having any school friends suggest to everybody I meet now that I was? Probably. Probably best not to think about it. Could always go on Facebook and see if anybody wants to hook up. That's a non-starter Danny and you know it. What about a Facebook for dogs? A place where pets can keep in touch after they've moved. Some stupid American woman has probably already set that up. Can just imagine the squeaky voice she puts on when she pretends her dog's talking. Those people do us more harm than good. Where do we stand then? Nineteen hundred to one. By the end of tomorrow that'll be nineteen hundred to two. Jesus Christ you'll never break even at this rate. Enough. You're a young man Danny, you've got time on your side. I pick up a cart that's been knocked over and add it to the rest. That's me, got a whole line of trolleys, time to snake my way inside the store. Let a woman with a kid nip in front, smile at them, no rush, this is better than the grocery department, less pressure. See Mark over at the Customer Services chatting with Sara and Margaret. If it wasn't for him thinking that he's somehow got one over on me this job would be perfect. Sara and Margaret give a big laugh at something he says just as I pass. They better not be laughing at me. No fucking way. Relax, you're just being paranoid Danny. No, I'm not. It's like if a woman suspects her husband's cheating on her he usually is. The same with cunts laughing at you.

—What you laughing at? I say.

Trying to sound innocent and not para but there is an edge to my voice I had hoped to hide. They turn to me. Sara and Margaret, both in their sixties. Margaret is clinically obese and Sara is balding. Eighth wank material.

—In Alaska they have a lottery only for the Eskimos, Sara says.

That's my joke, that's my fuckin' joke.

—You have to be Inuit to win it! Margaret says.

And they both start laughing again while Mark shrugs and gives me a little smile.

—How do you like being a trolley boy? he says.

OK, tough guy, I can play games too.

—Love it, I say.

You didn't expect that, did you ya prick? Not really playing games if I'm being honest. I do enjoy the freedom but still.

—That's a pity because –

—You'd have to pay me to go back to grocery.

—Well obviously. Nobody works here for free Danny, Mark says.

Sara and Margaret laugh and this time at me for sure. I start moving off. Need some fresh air. Hide round the back for five minutes and chat to Ronnie doing the deliveries.

—Where you going? Mark says.

—Outside to get more trolleys. Some of us take our jobs seriously y'know and not as an excuse to giggle and waste company time.

Christ I hope no-one else heard me say that. The two old yins seem a bit put out.

—You're going nowhere, Mark says.

It's ambiguous and intentionally so. How dare this cunt say that to me? But what you gonna do about it Danny? Nothing, as per usual. Next time. It's always fucking next time.

—You're back on grocery, he says. —Change and then start on ten to fourteen.

As I walk onto aisle fourteen Joanne is working a box of biscuits, lazily putting them on the shelf. She glances up as I near.

—Look who it is, she says.

Oh great… but she does smile. She may be taking the piss or about to have a breakdown. I have no idea, not after the last time.

—Do you like poetry? she says.

Fuckin' hell. What new devilry is this?

—Em…

—I wrote a poem last night, she says.

This must be an attack. Nobody could be that brave. But she is seventeen.

–Good for you.

–It's called *Pavlov's Cat*.

I nod. Wheels within wheels, riddles within riddles.

–Do you get it? she says.

–I understand the words if that's what you mean.

Trying to find the trick but can't. What is she after?

–What do you think?

–You've just told me the title.

–I know. But what do you think?

Sometimes the mouse does not eat the cheese. Sod her.

–I think you should do another one and call it *Schrodinger*'s *Dog*.

She stares at me.

–I thought you were different, she says.

And walks off.

Had to get out of my flat, even if only for an hour. Was developing something that looked like a bed sore on my back. Plus the paranoia. Not good. So here I am. Queen's Park. Sitting on a bench overlooking a small pond. Ducks. Bit cold. Wish I'd brought a rug. Jesus Danny, why not go the whole way and get a pipe too? What you really need is a crossbow and a mask – Whoa, relax. Just breath. Feel the sun. Watch the ducks. I like ducks. Should have bought a loaf, no, that's bad for them. I wonder if there's a pet shop about… There's the guy again, didn't I see him earlier? He's older than me, forty maybe, and even though I don't want to I can't help glancing at him. Why is he just standing there? Either take a seat or keep moving pal. But he doesn't. Fuck it, I was enjoying those ducks too. I get up and start walking. There are other benches. At the top of the hill you sometimes see squirrels, I'll go there and if he follows… Oh shit he's moving. MI5, he must be, the old guy outside B&Q and now this? It all adds up. Wait a second, he's cut off up a different path. Paranoia Danny. Don't let it build. That's what they want. Everything is designed to make you feel insecure. To make you feel doubt, to force you into a life of doing nothing. Climate change and global warming. It seems cut and dried but then there was that documentary about sun spots and the planet's natural weather cycles and how some people are making a helluva lot of money out of wind farms and if you even bring up the fact that it might not be so simple to some people they bite your head off which makes you think there's something fishy going on. Thatcher was well into global warming and that's enough on its own to instil doubt even though she was doing it to piss off the miners. Doubt means you won't act, or won't act with conviction which is pretty much the same. So they've won and you feel bad. Keep things black and white. They hate that. Yes or no. To be a cunt or not to be a cunt. That is the only real question that matters and every other question comes down to it in the end. Doubt is the real enemy, doubt is the weapon that they use the most. Pretend you know what you're doing even if you haven't a clue.

Come to a fork in the path, there he is, the guy again, coming towards me. Have to act quickly and turn back the way I came. Okay, this is it, paranoia or bust. I walk off the path and into a wooded part of the park and if I see him now then he must be MI5. Look, a squirrel – there he is! Closing in on me. Consider running but fuck this I'm not doing anything wrong and if he's looking for a fight he's got one.

—What do you want? I say.

—What do you want? he says.

—I want you to tell me what you want!

—Tell me what you want first? he says.

What the fuck?

—Look, what's going on here? I say.

—I haven't a clue, you were the one giving me the come on, he says.

Oh thank God, he's gay! Could almost kiss him.

—I thought you were MI5, I say.

—Oh shit, are there police about? he says.

—No, I mean, I thought you were following me.

—I was following you.

I laugh, this is funny. He laughs too.

—I'm John, he says.

—Danny, I say.

And then I don't know why but we end up shaking hands.

—So what happens now? he says.

A moment of silence. His hand goes to the belt on his jeans.

—I think I'm going to go home and have my tea, I say, —I've got some reduced to clear vegetable lasagne that needs to be eaten.

—Do you want to suck my cock? he says.

—Em, no thank you –

—Do you want me to suck your cock?

—You're alright, listen, I'd best see to this lasagne, cheerio.

Turn my back and start to walk away. He follows.

—Is that it? he says.

I don't stop but he's right behind me.

—Trust me I'd be hopeless at it anyway, I say.

—What? he says.

—It's like the story about the American soldiers pissing on the bodies of the Taliban, I say.

—What?

—I could never have done that because I can't even pee with other men about so there's not much chance of being able to do anything else.

Oh my God I'm babbling now but he's not giving up, almost at my side.

—What? he says.

—Look, there's been a bit of a misunderstanding, I say, –I'm sorry.

—Why were you coming on to me then? he says.

—I wasn't.

—Yes you were. You kept making eyes at me and then led me into the woods.

—I've said I'm sorry mate.

—How sorry? he says.

No point keeping this going so I do a quick sprint out of the woods towards the path.

—You're a cock teaser, he calls after me.

I don't answer and make it to the trail, a family, mum, dad and two wee girls on bikes, surprised as I burst out of the woods. Please don't follow, please don't follow. And then I hear a shout.

—Cock teaser! That's what you are!

I smile at the dad and shake my head like this has got nothing to do with me. John appears, a leaf stuck to his hair.

—You can't run forever, he shouts.

Break into a jog past the family, the dad putting a protective arm around his youngest as I pass but John's not giving up and then he's right next to me.

—Go away, I say.

—No Danny, we need to talk about this.

—I'm not gay, I say.

—I'm not either, he says. –I just like giving blowjobs.

And that fucking family are there again and they can all just fuck off because the way they're looking at us you'd think we were criminals.

—It's natural to be scared, he says.

And that's all it takes and I start to cry and John puts his arms around me and I'm hoping that it's only his belt I'm feeling but I try not to think about it and hug him tighter.

—Are you okay? he says.

—I'm a killer, I say.

—What?

—I'm a killer.

He pulls away. Turns his back and then runs as fast as he can. Start chasing after him for a second because I was really enjoying that hug then realise this is crazy and it's time to go home and back to bed.

6

Christ it's early, not even 6am yet. Still some stragglers on the street who've obviously been out clubbing the night before but I'm sober so can dodge them without making it seem like I'm dodging them – key to this is seeing them far enough away and that's when you change to the other side of the road, do it too close and you're asking for trouble. Also, beginning to run when you see a beggar as if you're about to catch a bus can work marvels, and that's what I do now, flitting past the down-and-out I missed hidden in the doorway who was just about to open his mouth. I *am* about to catch a bus so we'll pretend that one was legit. Cross over the grass and I'm at the car park. At one end I can see the minibus and a few guys milling about, including Stevie. The head of the hunt saboteurs, Stevie's one of the good guys, heart in the right place and all but there's something about him I just don't like. No sign of Shona. Shit. She's got to come today. At least Seb's here.

—Stevie, how you doing? I say.
He shakes his head.
—Not too good actually, he says.
Nip this in the bud I think.
—Great. Alright Seb?

Seb nods and holds up a small digital camera. I take it off him, whoa, it's quality gear.

—This is like totally top of the range man. How could you afford it on your student loan?

He gives a little embarrassed shrug as I hand it back to him. I get it. It's not only animals he liberates.

—I've never been on a fox hunt before. What should I do? Seb says.

And there's a slight waver in his voice and I can tell that he needs reassuring. He really does look up to me. I knew it. Even after the last time... That's touching, that's fucking touching and I feel my eyes start to well up but manage to hide it with a sniff and to make it totally believable wipe my nose with the sleeve of my jacket.

—These fox hunting bastards are real scum, I say.
I point to the camera.

—That's our protection. If they know they're being filmed they won't try to hit us quite so much. You got a really important job there, Seb.

—But what exactly should I film?

Time for a wry laugh and can't help but raise my voice slightly so that everybody hears.

—If you're ever unsure about where to point that thing just focus in on me, I'm always right in the thick of it.

Am I a total arsehole? The thought suddenly hits home and I can feel a sweat coming on. One of the others, a bloke I don't know, butts in.

—Most of them are over six foot, he says.
Where'd that come from?

—Yeah, that's true. Big bastards, I say.

—Cause of all the meat they eat. That's how you can tell. Anyone over six foot. Fuckin' murderer. For women it's five foot five.

Yep, another weirdo. I nod but when he turns away I shake my head at Seb. Glance over to see if she's coming. She's not but Paul is, walking kinda hunched with his right hand covering the side of his face. Not talked to him since the night at the strip club. Act like it never happened.

—Huh, Paul says.

He doesn't move his hand but up close his eyes look even more bloodshot than mine. No point beating about the bush. His hand is over his face, it's impossible to pretend there's nothing funny going on. Plus, it is only Paul.

—What's up with your face? I say.

Everybody is staring at him, some outright, others through the corners of their eyes. He lowers his hand.

—Ahh! we all shriek.

A piece of twisted plastic is lodged in his cheek and slightly protrudes from a pool of pus. The whole side of his face is one giant white head.

—None of you bastards heard of sensitivity? Paul says.

—Holy shit man, what happened? I say.

—Last week I was passing this car and there was a dog inside and all the windows were rolled up and the wee fucker was passed out on the seat, hardly breathing. I checked for the owners, couldn't see them, got a brick and put the window in. Bastard dog sprang into life and fuckin' attacked me. Piece of the plastic lining from the window got caught in its teeth as it bit my face off and ended up stuck in my cheek.

That isn't funny Danny, don't laugh.

—Seriously Paul, you should go to the hospital, I say.

—I did. They said it would be best to leave it and let the plastic make its own way out.

Seb, who's staring in fascination and even with his scarf covering his mouth, you can tell it's open in amazement, suddenly points at the piece of plastic.

—I think I saw it move just then!

—Of course it moves when I'm talkin' ya fuckin' idiot.

Paul looks caught between wanting to cry and wanting to kill someone.

—Are you sure you're up for today? I say.

—I've been locked up in my flat all week, he says. —I was going crazy. And you know how I feel about foxes. I love those cunts.

That's good enough for me. Who'd have thought Paul was a man of integrity?

—You're bang on Paul, I'll say that about you.

Stevie checks his watch and calls over.

—Danny, it's getting late. I think this is all we're getting.

—No, give it another minute or two.

I've got everything I'm going to say to her planned word for word. I can make things better. All she has to do is be here.

—Oh, I see. We're waiting for the crazy bitch, Paul says.

Fuck this freak.

—She's not crazy and she's not a bitch. Take that back.

—Oh aye Danny, she's perfectly normal. I wonder what she'll be dressed as today?

—Maybe she'll have a spare balaclava you can borrow, Seb says.

That's worth a huge guffaw and even though I know it's bad form I laugh excessively.

—Nice one Seb.

I can see Stevie's getting impatient, he's not gonna hold on much longer. Wait a second. There she is, in green camouflage gear but without the balaclava, which would be a step in the right direction if it wasn't for the man beside her dressed exactly the same with his hand floating dangerously close to her arse.

—Shona, I say.

She nods at me and Seb and without saying a word pulls out a balaclava and offers it to Paul. He turns away, hiding his face, and heads into the bus. She places a hand on the arm of the guy she's with.

—This is Jason. He's got more experience than all of us put together.

—Hi, Seb says. —Pleased to meet you.

What's he playing at being super friendly to this prick?

—I've got quite a bit of experience myself, I say.

Jason looks at me and I look back. Can't keep it up and end up lowering my eyes. Brilliant, he's not even said a word and already I'm relegating myself to yesterday's man. Bastard shouldn't be with her anyway, he must be about thirty. What is it with old guys going out with girls a lot younger than them?

—It's time to go, Stevie says.

And we pile into the back.

Sitting beside Paul was never part of the plan. And with the hole in his face angled my way thank God I didn't have breakfast. Seb's to my left playing with his phone, looks expensive, must have come from the same place he got the camera. Across from me are Jason and Shona. There's a small rucksack wedged between his legs that he's keeping a hold of even though he seems to be dozing. Shona's eyes are closed and I take the opportunity to get a really good stare in. The short hair is growing on me and I've got to admit she looks healthy, a lot healthier than I do. Maybe going nuts is the smart play. Trying not to over-think today's expedition but have secretly made a deal with myself that if we (I) can save the fox then I'll be able to move on from the lab rescue disaster. Feeling a bit edgy and it's not just because Jason's suddenly appeared. Internal monologues getting closer and closer to making an appearance on the outside. Just hope it doesn't happen at work. Or right now. Shona moves her head and rests it on Jason's shoulder, simultaneously waking him up and making him tighten his grip on the rucksack. There's something in there. Fucker's probably brought sandwiches and a thermos.

   —So where did you meet Shona? I say.

   —What? Jason says.

   —You and Shona. How did you get together?

What the fuck am I doing? Trying to set them up? Half expect him to think about what I said, nod to himself before nudging her and asking her to marry him.

   —She came along to this group I'm part of. I was really impressed by her.

   —What's this group then? I say.

Go on, say it's for men without penises.

   —It's a secret, he says.

Could be...

   —But it's not for little pussies who think that chaining themselves to a McDonalds is pretty hard.

... But probably not. He leans back before turning to look out of the window. Shona snuggles closer into him. Paul, also asleep but not quite so angelic, rolls over and his head moves onto my lap wound-side down, the impact making the sound your foot does in a puddle. I'd just washed those trousers as well.

The minibus stops at a lay-by on a country road. Shona comes to and stretches. Paul isn't moving, his face melting onto my thighs. From the front Stevie flings me and a few of the others air horns.

— Make sure you're close to the hunt when you sound them off. If we're too far away then we run the risk of sending the fox back in their direction.

Jason gives Shona a horn and they share a little smile. He gives her the horn. Subtext becoming the text. Know it's bad but can't help myself. Let the air horn off in Paul's ear.

— WAAAA!

In the cramped confines of the bus the sound is blinding. Paul wakes terrified and peels himself from my lap while everybody else (barring Seb, good lad) stares at me disapprovingly.

— Fuckssake Danny!

— I was just checking that it worked, I say.

Sod them. I open the back door and am first out. There's nine of us in total. Wait a second. I've not been switched on today at all. There's only fucking nine of us.

— Where's the rest?

Stevie sighs.

— Yeah... cause it's banned, it's harder to get people interested.

This is bad news, even with three times this number it's still hit or miss.

—We should split into two groups, give us a better chance of ruining it for them, Stevie says.

Ok, once more into the breach. Step forward Danny Boy.

—Who wants to go with me?

That could have come out better. Borderline 'who likes me?' statement. Forget about it, it's done now. What a surprise, nobody moves in my direction. Eyeball Seb and Paul.

—Come on, I hiss.

And they do, Paul dragging his feet. What's Shona doing? Looking at Jason of course. Fuck. He nods at her and she heads over to join us. You'd think if you were happy and sad at the same time they'd cancel each other out and you'd reach an equilibrium not a suicidal rage. Kill yourself with a real element of vindictiveness. Choose torture not sleeping pills. The others fall in with Stevie. Jason hands the rucksack to Shona before joining them. He's made her lunch. I've got to admit that's smooth.

—Come and get your map Danny, Stevie says.

I stand beside him and follow his finger as he outlines the path we should take. I hate maps.

—If you follow the gully all the way up –

—That's a gully?

—Yeah... Danny, you know that the circular lines represent altitude –

—Oh yeah, I know that. We go up the gully, that's fine. That's all you needed to say.

I wander back to the rest still studying the map but already lost.

—Any of you know anything about maps? It's a fuckin' joke – Stevie cuts me off with a shout.

—Good luck Danny. You got a camera yeah? Ok then. We'll see you back here when it's all over.

He and his group move off through a hedge into a field. I study the map. Not a clue. I might as well be trying to translate the Rosetta Stone and I'm just about to point in a random direction when Shona stops me from making a total arse of myself.

—This way, she says.

Seb and Paul look at me but I'm already following her so they do the same. I catch her up and we walk abreast for a few moments. Last thing I should do is enquire about him, that'd be desperate.

—You know that guy Jason well or... ?

—Well enough, she says.

Another few strides to think. Getting lost is becoming a habit.

—What does that mean? Shona, y'know, you don't want to go out with me, that's fine, I'm not going to lose sleep over it (well done son, you said that with a straight face). But that guy, I think he's dodgy.

Shona shakes her head at me like I'm a kid.

—We're not romantically entwined Danny. It's just, him and his friends. They get the job done.

Nod but unsure of what that means. We continue in silence. Tempted to say something hurtful to Paul simply to break the tension but don't have the energy. It's one of those days when the air is thick with moisture and even though it's not raining you're gonna get soaked right through anyway. Take a deep breath and hold it in. Feel better for it and perk up, realise I'd zoned out for the last few minutes and we're coming up to a bend in the road. Clip-clop. The sound of horse's hooves on tarmac. Stride forward and take the lead, almost say 'I'm on point' but after the last time I've realised that using military terms makes me sound like a total twat. Still fifty metres away from the bend when a lone horseman comes into view. Big bugger on the horse, dressed in the red and white of a huntsman, a riding crop in his hand that looks like it could do a lot of damage. We've stopped but he hasn't, getting closer with a little sneer on his puffed red face and heading straight for us. Cheeks so red they could be rouged, like a clown's. Like clowns. Clowns. No Danny, not here, not again.

—That guy was right. He is over six foot, Seb says.

He sounds frightened and that's all I need for the fraternal instinct to kick in.

—Get on the camera Seb. I'll handle this.

The rider's still on a collision course but fucked if I'm moving and he pulls up just short.

—Ha! I didn't know it was Halloween already! I say.

I indicate his comical dress. Nothing, not a chuckle. The enemy within, it's always the same. I turn round to face Seb and Paul.

—I know it wasn't funny but you could laugh. What's going on here isn't about comedy.

That must have come across really pathetic but fuck it, they were in the wrong, and I almost forget the rider as I'm thinking about what am I doing here with people who don't even laugh at my jokes when the horse barges into my back.

—What you playing at ya wanker!

Stumble but just manage to keep my feet. That was close. And now he's closer, leaning towards me.

—I'm a wanker eh! Well you're scum! And scum has to be dealt with my lad!

What century has this fucker come from? And then he's raising his hand with the crop and I have to dodge as he lashes out.

—What you doing? We've got a camera! I shout.

Look for Seb and see him recording at the same time the rider does. He's about to kick his heels in when he jerks from his saddle and falls to the ground, his flesh making a slapping sound as it hits the tarmac, Shona suddenly visible behind him. His wrist is bent at a funny angle and I move forward to see what I can do but Shona beats me to it except instead of helping she's picked up the riding crop and is laying into him. He's covering up in a ball and makes the mistake of instinctively raising his broken arm to protect his face and takes the brunt of the crop on his wrist. It's left dangling. He's screaming and I feel sick but Shona's cool as fuck and puts the air horn to the horse's ear. Lets off a blast and it bolts down the road. She starts walking away as if nothing's happened. I look over to Seb and Paul and see that Seb has filmed the whole thing.

—Shit. Give me the SD card Seb.

He hands it over. I try to snap it in two with my hands but can't and fling it to the ground and stamp on it. The rider's thrown up over himself. Shona's up ahead about to get out of sight but I feel bad about leaving.

—You alright pal? Bit of a nasty sprain there eh?

Right angles. His wrist is at a fucking right angle. He doesn't say anything and dry baulks.

—Ok then. See you later.

Give Seb and Paul the nod and we break into a jog. Shona gives me a smile when we catch her up.

—What was that all about? I say.

—He knew the risks. In war there are always casualties.

—But Seb had him with the camera! For fuckssake Shona –

She stops and so do I.

—I can't believe you're defending him.

—I'm not defending him but he could have broken his neck falling off the horse –

—So?

So. So what? The answer that is impossible to counter and suddenly I'm on the back foot.

—Well...

—So? she says again.

—Well then we're entering a whole grey area. We're about saving animals not killing people. It's best to stick with what you know.

—And what do you know Danny? she says.

Oh Christ I didn't know there'd be questions. Think for a few seconds and we reach the moment in a conversation when there's been a long enough silence to signify its end. She turns her back on me.

—I know that it's wrong to be cruel to animals, I say.

But she doesn't look round, sighs instead, and I feel like I've just said something stupid which is rich when you consider what we're doing. This is rapidly turning into another disaster and the thought of packing it all in enters my mind for a second before the sound of a hunting horn in the distance is enough to bring me back. That guy had it coming. Fuck him. I punch Seb on the shoulder.

—Ok. This is it. We got a fox to save. We're gonna forget what happened just then. Remember, we're a team. We're here for the animals. Let's do this.

Shona starts walking in the opposite direction from where the horn came from.

—Where you going?

—I've got my own plans, she says.

—But we're supposed to head off the hunt. How you gonna do that over there?

—I don't have time for this. You can try to stop the hunt if you like. I'm dealing with the bigger picture.

—What bigger picture? We're supposed to be a fuckin' team! She shrugs and continues on her way. Thank God I don't have abandonment issues.

—Fine. Do what you want.

I turn to Paul and Seb, at least they're not deserting me.

—What we waiting for then? Let's go.

—Next time can I go in the other group? Paul says.

—No you fucking well can't.

Shit. Glance behind me and already she's out of sight.

—Fuck it. You two go ahead.

I double back and run after her. No sign of Shona on the road but then see her in the field alongside. I climb over a stone wall and get to her when she's a third of the way across. I slow down to walk beside her but she doesn't even acknowledge my presence.

—You gonna at least let me know where we're going?

She points at a location on the map.

—You know I can't read maps, I say.

—You're hopeless, Danny, she says.

Think of all the women Norman Wisdom pulled in his films by being pathetic. Times must have changed because the chances of getting a blowjob out of pity in this day and age are exactly zero. Not that I would accept a pity blowjob anyway. Well, it would depend.

—If I'm hopeless think how much more hopeless you are than me. I mean, I'm here to look after you, I say.

—I didn't ask you to come, she says.

—Where we going anyway?

—The Manor.

—What we doing there?

—Gonna pay our respects, she says.

Since when did Shona start talking like Clint Eastwood? Oh yeah, I know since when. We trudge along in silence and it's getting muddier and I've totally the wrong footwear on so that's these shoes and the trousers that Paul leaked onto ruined forever. This hunt is costing me a fortune.

    —You know how you said you didn't want to talk about what happened with the dogs on the roof... You still that way inclined or... ?

She doesn't answer and I get the message. Sense that I've pissed her off.

    —Good. I'm glad you're over it. I am too. Had a good laugh about it the other day in work.

She glances at me and I see anger in her eyes but she controls herself and walks on.

    —What do you mean laugh about it? she says.

    —Y'know what they say, if you don't laugh you'd cry.

Shit. It was bad idea bringing it up because all I can see is Norman (the dog, not Wisdom) going over the edge and if today doesn't work out I'm fucked I really am. But at least she's ignoring me and as we plod on I feel her anger receding and the tension lightening. A distance away I can make out the shape of the Manor House but Shona leads us at a slight angle from it to the top of a small hill overlooking the road that leads into the grounds. She crouches and pulls out a mobile phone.

    —Who you calling? I say.

    —No one. Get down.

I kneel beside her as she studies a text before putting the mobile away.

—Good news?

—Jason should be here any second.

Ask a stupid question. Silence, more uncomfortable for me than for her, and just to break it I open my mouth.

—Can I use your phone?

—What for?

—I want to call my mum.

And as soon as I say it I know it was a mistake and although she smiles at me it's even more patronising than earlier and I preferred the scowl. She hands me the phone and I punch in the numbers. Will have to make this quick.

—Hi mum, it's me.

Jason appears from nowhere and hunkers down in between us. Where'd he come from?

—What's he doing? Jason says.

—Phoning his mother, Shona says.

—I'm fine mum, just about tomorrow, I don't know if I'll be able to make it, I say.

Jason points at the Manor.

—That's where the bastards are, he says.

He's talking to Shona but I know he's talking loudly to embarrass me and I want to hang up but now she's into a story about one of her friends having cancer and I can't leave her like this.

—Evil fuckers, all of them, Jason says.

Mum heard that.

—No it was nothing mum. Go on, what were you saying? I say.

—**Cunt City**, Jason practically shouts next to my ear and I hang up as my mum says the words *hair loss*.

—You did that on purpose.

—Did I? he says.

This guy's making a big fuckin' mistake in underestimating me. I've not reached the point where I'm so low I can't even over-compensate.

—Maybe you should wait here Danny. It's gonna heat up from now on in, he says.

—Don't even think about it pal, I'm staying with Shona. One of us has got to have some common sense.

Jason shrugs and places an arm around her. He points at the Manor.

—It's time we got in there.

She nods but that's not what's got my attention. That arm is out of bounds. This isn't jealousy, this is feminism by proxy. I prod him in the back.

—Watch what you're doing with that arm pal.

Oh yeah, this'll impress her.

—What?

—Her personal space. You're infringing it.

His arm stays where it is, squeezes slightly.

—I don't need you to decide what's an infringement of my personal space or not, Shona says.

—Oh, ok, sorry, it's just I thought you said you two weren't romantically involved, I say.

—Romance is dead, Shona says.

—Well young lady you've just talked yourself out of a Valentine's card, I say.

Trying to crack shit jokes in the middle of an argument is an admission that you've lost. Jason grits his teeth but it looks fake, like he's practiced being furious in front of the mirror.

—If there's anyone infringing personal space here it's you.

You're not wanted Danny. Beat it.

He rises to his feet, tugging Shona at the same time.

—Come on.

She follows him without giving me a second glance. They head down the hill and away. You're not wanted Danny. It's funny how at the end of the day when it comes to making people feel bad it's always the simple things that work best. *You're ugly, you're stupid, you're useless.* Remember as a kid, Primary three maybe, being left out by the rest of the class for some game and chasing them as if that was what we'd wanted to play all along. The whole question of whether it's better to be part of a group of total arseholes or be on your own. Age helps with that one. The world is split between cunts and bastards, the bastards being the best that humanity can offer and the cunts being the cunts. Now the cunts outnumber the bastards by about twenty to one so even if you somehow manage to spot the cunts (which is tricky as cunts do a good job of disguising the fact) and surround yourself with bastards there is still one central problem – you are surrounded by bastards. I can see Jason and Shona enter the Manor grounds and then turn up the drive and out of sight. You're not wanted Danny. Where I am feels pretty good (out of the wind and the grass fairly dry) and just crashing here seems like an idea. Try to fill my mind with images of animal pain and torture to get something moving inside but the usual triggers aren't working. Could so easily go to sleep. Need to get up and help Shona but know deep down that the only people I save are in my dreams and even that's beginning to change. The dream I had last night, a fire somewhere, I wasn't one of the major players, a fireman or trapped Steve McQeen type figure, just a member of the crowd watching at the fringes and didn't have a good view as I was at the back and there was this whole queuing system that I didn't understand. Woke up before I was told how it had finished. Right, this isn't doing anyone any good. If you don't watch out you'll be here forever. You asked for this Danny. Disney Films. Fucking talking animal, fucking wisecracking cows, fucking Disney Films. Cunts eating hotdogs while watching *Sharks* discussing vegetarianism. That's gotta be linked to *if not the root of* every fucking problem on the planet. *The Lion King* leads to pensioners getting raped and one of these days I'll prove it to the world. That's better and I'm up and heading down the slope. Fuck Jason I'm getting Shona. She's my friend and you don't desert your friends. Can feel heat inside me and it's good and now I'm through the gates and on the road to the Manor House. Panic for a second because I can't see them but there they are, heading to the left down a stone path. I catch them up and Jason grimaces at me but I feel like I've overcome something inside and blow him a kiss which was probably a mistake but at least Shona didn't see it. Almost a bit light headed, going to have to watch myself. We pass under some trees and then we're in a garden, a lot bigger and a lot more ornate than a normal garden, but a garden nonetheless.

—We're here, Jason says.

—What's this? We gonna steal some shrubs? I say.

They both ignore me and Jason points to a large headstone in a far corner that I'd missed.

—That's what we're after.

They head over and I'm still not sure what's going on but now notice other headstones scattered about but blending in with the garden so you could easily overlook them. Not bad. Your own personal graveyard. Jason gets on his knees, opening his bag at the graveside. If he's got sandwiches he better share them cause I'm starving. The marble headstone is extravagantly sculpted and on it are the words:

William Talbot III – 1793–1851 – Thirteenth Earl of Talbot. Shona's down beside Jason and he pulls out two small hand shovels, one for her, and they both start digging into the turf. So it wasn't food then.

—You've got to be kidding, I say.

I lean down and take Shona's arm.

—We're leaving.

She pushes me away and I try again and this time she slaps my hand but does at least look at me.

—This family have been hunting and killing for hundreds of years. Thousands of animals have died. Their hands are red with blood. Today we're gonna go some way towards evening the score.

—How does digging up the bones of their ancestors even the score?

Jason stops what he's doing and turns to me like I'm a moron.

—We don't just dig up the bones. We send them the skull covered in animal shit and a note with our demands. Understand now?

—You've convinced me. Got another shovel?

He points to the bag.

—There's one in there.

—I wasn't being fuckin' serious man! Shona, this isn't right. But she isn't paying any attention to me and I look back the way we came to the Manor House. On a day like today there'll be a helluva lot of people about. Big angry people who are fox hunting even though it's banned.

—Y'know, if they catch you doing this you'll be in real trouble.

It's no good. I'm the invisible man. Fuck. But I can't leave her and this time I'm not joking.

—Where's the shovel? I say.

Jason flings his at me and gets the spare for himself. I crouch down beside them and get to work. It's been wet the last few days which is lucky for us and while it's not exactly knife through butter it's surprising how deep we get in a comparatively short time. The key to this is getting into a rhythm so it doesn't seem like you're straining yourself. Do a quick check, yep, I'm sweating the most followed by Shona then Jason. Bastard's taking it easy. About five feet down we're having to stand and use our heels on the handles to get the earth moving. Far away I think I hear the sound of a hunting horn.

—Did you hear that?

—What? Shona says.

–The hunt must be close by, I say.

—So? Jason says.

Just my luck, another professional debater.

—So if they're close by they might get closer and if they get closer they might see us and if they see us they won't find this funny.

—It's not supposed to be funny, Jason says.

I start to reply but decide it'd be better not to waste my breath and keep digging, fear giving me an extra burst. Bang. There it is, the coffin. I pull back and this is the only time Jason takes the initiative.

—Move, he says.

I get out the way and he starts scraping the remaining earth from the lid. It's still intact thank fuck but I look away anyway and with a shock realise how deep we are. The top of the grave is a good foot above my head and claustrophobia is in danger of making an appearance. Am definitely getting worse. Couldn't watch the Charles Bronson sections in *The Great Escape* last Christmas and that's a U for fuckssake. Spread my arms out and touch the earth walls and don't know whether it's real or in my head but they feel like they could give way any second. Completely swallowed by the fucking earth. Turn back to the coffin to bring me down and a part of me realises that if I'm using a coffin to stop from freaking out I must really be in the shit. Jason's almost done and the long rectangular box lies before us. Expect to see Shona's face change somehow but it's the same expression as before, just a little red from the exercise.

—She's first out, Jason says.

I nod and we propel her out of the grave and into the open air.

—Me next, I say.

I stick my foot out for a punt but he's turned away from me to lean over the coffin and I have to put my foot back down before I fall.

—Let's hurry the fuck up, I say.

Jason raises his shovel and slams it down on the coffin. The shovel breaks. Brilliant. Shona whistles and we both look up.

—I don't want to worry you or anything but I can hear horses, she says.

That's enough for me, sure I can feel the walls begin to reverberate. Speed is of the essence.

—Out the way, I say.

I draw the shovel up above my head and hit the coffin as hard as I can. My shovel splits in two.

—Fuck! That's it. Let's go. I told you this was a bad idea.
Jason shakes his head. Shona drops to the grass above us and
lies flat dropping her head into the hole.

—I think they're coming, she says.
And I can hear the sound of hooves as well. Jesus Christ if they
find us like this they'll bury us alive.

—What can we do? Shona says.

—Run like fuck, I say.
But she's not talking to me. Jason takes a long look at the coffin
and nods to himself.

—We'll steal the coffin. Get some rope.
Shona disappears to look in her bag, but this I cannot take.

—You've got to be kidding this time! We cannot nick the
    fuckin' coffin! If they catch us lugging that about they'll
    string us up.

—We need the skull, Shona says.
And the rope falls at my feet. When I said it earlier I didn't
actually believe it but I really am the only one here with any
common sense and that thought alone is enough to bring on
another wave of terror.

—You want the skull? I'll get you the fuckin' thing if it
    means we can get away from here. Help me up.
Jason doesn't look like he believes me but lets me get on his
shoulders and Shona pulls me out. Open air breath it in. Feel a
bit calmer already and I should just go.

—What's your plan? Shona says.
But not without her. Look back down into the grave. Jason's
sitting on the coffin. Unbelievable.

—Get off the coffin.
He stands up and squeezes himself against the earth. I take

another deep breath and jump two-footed into the air and down, my feet crashing against – and through – the coffin lid.

—Ahh!

A shard of wood, please God be wood, digs into my ankle and I can feel the skin being scraped back and I think it's at the bone but if it really was the pain wouldn't let me think. Want to collapse but I'm not hitting the deck where I stand, something is crunching underfoot, and I hop out of the coffin and fall against the crumbling graveside.

—Danny? You ok? Shona says.

The light-headedness is back and it's a good thing I didn't have anything to eat because if I did it'd be making an encore. Jason's stooped over the coffin and I don't want to look but it's going to happen anyway so best get it over with and through the window of torn wood I see the bones of the deceased aristocrat open for public viewing. A green mould covers half of the skull and Jason's acting like Indiana Jones poised over it with open hands. But not the real Indiana Jones, the Indiana Jones if they'd got Tom Selleck to do it like they initially wanted. As in shite.

—What you waiting for? I say.

Jason grabs it and flings it to Shona in one motion. The skull's still attached to part of the spine and there's a good two foot or so long tail stuck to the back of the head as it flies through the air. She catches it, puts her hand on the spine and with a jerk snaps it from the skull. Fuck me. Still too stunned and hurt to make a move and can only stay where I am as Jason uses me as a step ladder and with Shona's help gets out of the grave, kicking at the earth for leverage and chunks of it landing beside me. Gets out of the grave. I'm the only one left in here and thanks to that cunt the walls are caving in.

—Put it in your bag, Jason says to Shona.

Their voices are faint and getting fainter and I can't see either of them and please God this isn't happening.

—Fuckin' get me out of here!

—In a minute, Jason says.

But I'm not staying. I can't die like this. Nobody's helping me and the panic is overriding everything and I try to pull myself up but the earth is giving way and I somehow manage to get a single crumbling foothold and propel my head above the grave for a split second and see their backs before falling back down. Another few frantic scrambling attempts end in failure and there's enough collapsed earth to rebury the coffin.

—Oi! a new voice, from a distance.

Oh please God no.

—Somebody! Help me! I shout.

Jason pokes his head into the grave and seeing even his face is a relief.

—Could you please be quiet? he says.

Then he disappears to continue his conversation with Shona. This bastard gives cunts a bad name.

—I'm getting buried alive!

Shona finally leans over with her hand outstretched and so does Jason thanks to her guilting him into it but all I care about is getting out of the pit and I'm beginning to hyperventilate as they haul me up. Suck in the air and glance around. No sign of the man whose voice I heard but he must be out there.

—I'll set off some smoke bombs along the way to buy you some time, Jason says to Shona.

Uh-oh. I need to get up to speed.

—Who's got the skull? I say.

Can hear muffled voices, there's people close by but I can't see shit because of the trees.

—Good luck, Jason says.

Shona clutches the bag she's holding. A bag with something making a bulge inside.

—Ho! Wait a fuckin' second, I say.

I grab Jason's arm.

—She's not taking the skull. It was your idea. You fuckin' take it.

He pushes me away and Shona steps in between us.

—This has nothing to do with you Danny, she says.

—It fuckin' well does. If you get caught with that they'll kill you.

She looks like she couldn't care less and it's true. She couldn't care less if she lived or died. I managed not to cry in the grave but this is pushing me close. It's my fault. All this is because of me.

—Give me the skull then, I say.

—No. This is what I came here to do.

Jason steps away from us to get a better view of the path we came in.

—They're here, he says.

Look over and see a group of six riders in the full red and white costume. They're just staring at us at the moment but it won't be long.

—Give it to me, I say.

—No.

I pretend to turn away but then lunge for the bag and grab it off her.

—It's mine now. Get going, I say.

—Danny!

She tries to take it from me but I hold it above my head and back off.

—I mean it, fuck off! I say.

She's still trying to snatch it from me and I stumble and almost fall back into the grave.

—What the bloody hell do you think you're doing?

It came from one of the riders and now they're on their way. They look pretty grim and I don't blame them. Three dodgy looking folk dressed in camouflage gear hanging around the recently excavated grave of your ancestor would piss anyone off. I push Shona in the direction of the trees where the horses won't be much use to them.

—Run!

She makes one last attempt for the bag but Jason pulls her away and they start for the cover. Immediately the riders head in their direction to block them off and there's no way they'll make it to safety in time. I shake myself. Not one rider is coming after me. Not one. Everybody's ignoring me today. I hold the bag up over my head and whistle. The riders turn their heads. I pull out the skull.

—I've got your granddaddy's head! Eh, what do you think about that?

They're not ignoring me anymore but I don't stay around to thank them. There's a stone wall about forty metres away in the opposite direction from Shona and that's all I've got in my mind. Glance round once and yep, they're all after me, no sign of her so she must have got away but no time to think cause I'm at the wall and in one jump over it – am I fuck – I fall back down and try again but there's nothing to hold on to and they're getting closer.

—Stay where you are!

Naw you're alright mate, lob the bag with the skull over the wall to free a hand and this time I make it and drop over the side. It's about a six foot fall but I'm up and on my feet before I even worry about being hurt. Seem ok although there's probably so much adrenaline in my body right now that if I got shot I'd probably be able to keep going for a few minutes like that clip they showed on the news years ago of a riot somewhere and a guy getting shot in the leg but still running even though it seemed impossible at the time. Can hear shouts from the other side of the wall but not interested. I'm in a field and on the far side it borders a wood and that's where I'm headed. Gotta keep focussed. Uneven ground and worse still water's collected in the ruts in the field so every second step or so my foot sinks in and sticks. Like running in a dream when your legs feel like glue but this is really happening and it's a total nightmare. My left foot goes in deeper than before and when I pull it out there's no trainer attached. Fuck. What was I thinking wearing these today? The wood's only another few strides but I have to stop and end up on my hands and knees trying to find my bloody shoe. There it is, don't bother putting it on just carry it and make it to the trees and at least the illusion of safety. Right. Put the trainer back on, it's full of mud and I have to scoop it out with my hand before I can get my foot in. Don't have a map and even if I did I wouldn't have a clue where I was but know I can't stay here. Feel a sob coming on and it's touch and go for a second but I manage to turn it into a laugh and that gives me some strength. Fuck em. Fuck em all. This could be the greatest moment of your life Danny and whatever you say this, *this* – getting chased by evil fuckers cause you've got their grandad's

skull – is definitely living, there's no argument about that. So forget the tears. You're alright son, this is what you were born to do. Through the trees and almost intentionally letting the branches hit my face cause pain's for the weak and it's like I've drunk an invulnerability potion. Let the rest of the world be obsessed with all the meaningless crap that's pumped through their TV screens, regurgitating celebrity gossip and memorising sports statistics. This is what I do for fun ya bunch of losers –
 —*Eieeeee!*
A horn. A fucking hunting horn close by and the fear is back twice as strong as before and if this is living you can keep it mate, turn to see if there's anyone on my tail and –
 —Ahh.
Fuckin' branch got me right in the face, that invulnerability potion didn't last long and the side of my mouth's cut and this time the sob escapes and it's no laughing matter. Got to get the fuck out of these trees and have to change direction a bit to where they're thinning. Don't feel tired but my breathing's all screwed and Jesus Christ I've slowed down and going not much faster than a quick walk. See a wall and a road beyond it and that's enough to give me a kick. Clear the trees and do the Green Cross Code. No one. Over the wall and onto the tarmac. SOPS. Standard Operating Procedures, never use common lines of transport in enemy territory. Sod it, those trees were freaking me out. Break into a jog. I need to find the minibus and get the hell out of Dodge. Round a corner and hang back just in case, shit, there's someone sitting on the side of the road... Doesn't look like a threat, he's got his head in his hands and I know that guy. I fuckin' know that guy! It's Paul! Run to him smiling and get a vision of two lovers coming together across a field

for some stupid reason and then I'm beside him and can't help myself and start to laugh.

—Thank God it's you Paul! Jesus Christ, I must have ran a couple of miles there. Shit.

I look back the way I've come and it hits me and I bend over double, panting, relief letting me level off. Ok. Feel better. Paul's not even looked up and his non-response is making me feel kinda embarrassed about being so high. This is no time for an uncomfortable moment.

—Listen up, we got a real situation on our hands.

—I'm not interested, he says.

—I wasn't interested either but I've ended up with some cunt's head! So stop fannying about, where is everybody?

He finally raises his eyes to mine and holy shit I'd forgotten about his face and it's even worse than before. The plastic's gone and instead there's a ragged hole, like a bullet that got as far as the cheek and then, feeling guilty about how much damage it had already done, decided to stop. Vagina cheek. Stop thinking these things Danny.

—Your plastic's out, I say. —Feeling better?

He ignores the question. Fair enough.

—What's in the bag? he says.

—The Thirteenth Earl of Talbot's skull. And they want it back, so help me out here. What's going on? We need to get to the bus.

He points to his cheek.

—Seb punched me.

—Oh. Why did he do that then?

But he's not listening to me and instead goes off on one as if it was me that hit him.

—Last week you were rescuing dogs from humans, this week you're rescuing foxes from dogs. What you got planned for next week Danny, saving chickens from foxes? It's a waste of time.

Only Paul could make today worse.

—There's a time and a place for this conversation –

—It was my birthday on Wednesday, he says, cutting me off.

—... Happy birthday.

—No, it wasn't actually. Y'see, I'm not twenty-five. I'm thirty-one.

—I never thought you were twenty-five, I say.

Where the fuck is this going?

—They check your passport. They check your fuckin' passport! he says.

—Who checks your passport?

—The reps! Don't you get it? I'll never be able to go on another Club 18–30 holiday again.

This is not happening this is not happening this is not happening.

—You don't get it, do you? he says. –You're one of them. This may shock you right, but I couldn't give a toss about animal rights. Nobody normal does. I was only in it cause I heard that the girls who were into this crap were slags. And they're not. At the end of the day there's only one kind of fox that can make you cum, and the other kind ain't worth saving.

Need to stay on track here, can't afford to be sidetracked, but holy fucking shit.

—I went back to the strip club to see Nicola, he says. –And do you know what she said?

—Fuck off Paul I don't have time for this.

—Yeah, that was pretty much it.

—Just tell me the direction the bus is in!

But he's not having any of it and pulls out an Organ Donor Card.

—I'm a registered Organ Donor. Must mean I'm some sort of hero don't you think?

Worse and worse and worse. He waves it in my face.

—Wouldn't you agree Danny? Good guy eh? Giving up his bits for the cripples?

—Whatever you say man but we got to prioritise here –

—I only carry this so that even in death there's a fifty percent chance I can get inside a woman.

I am going to die here. I am so definitely going to die here.

—I suppose you think I'm shallow, don't you? he says.

—The bus, quickly, where is it?

—I've got low self-esteem! Paul shouts.

—Keep it down for fuck's sake.

—Didn't you hear me?

He slumps.

—I've got low self-esteem, he says. –That's why I lie and cheat and take money from the collection tins, he says.

No, not this.

—You take money from the tins? But that money goes straight to the cat and dog home!

I half-heartedly raise a fist but we both know I'm not gonna use it and let it fall to my side.

—Low self-esteem, I say. –Everybody's got low self-esteem Paul. Even me, sometimes. But it's not an excuse.

He doesn't answer and hides his face. If he were an animal I'd feel sorry for him.

—Paul, there are people looking for me and if they find me they're gonna kill me. Tell me where the bus is. Please.

It doesn't look like he's gonna help but then he slowly raises his
arm to point and I'm off.

Middle of the road and running as fast as I can which isn't that
fast anymore but the best I can do. No pretence of trying to
keep out of sight. Got to make the bus. Get to the bus and I'm
safe. Not even thinking about it being gone. It'll be there and
it's up to me to be there too. I'm cold, the sweat making my
clothes stick to my skin. Think I can sense horses from the rever-
berations on the road but praying it's in my imagination. Turn
a bend and there it is – across a field I can see the minibus and
around it a cluster of people with their backs to me. Ya fuckin'
beauty. Either follow the road or take a short cut? So frightened
that they'll leave without me I'm heading for the field before
I'm consciously aware of what I'm doing, scratching myself on
the hedge as I squeeze through. One more push and that's me.
Sticking to the thicket to give me some protection and am almost
close enough to shout at them to wait and can make out Shona
and Jason and Seb and a couple of the others and think about
surprising them instead and how cool would that be? Won't
though and open my mouth to let them know I'm coming but
this time I definitely did hear the sound of horses from the road
on the other side of the hedge and I close my mouth without
making a sound. The minibus is only a hundred metres away,
just on the other side of a fence, and I can still make it, I'm
gonna make it, please don't leave, don't fucking leave, and that's
when I see them all pile in, Jason and Seb having to grab Shona
and pull her onboard. Try one last spurt but it's too much and
my legs are giving way and I collapse onto the earth only twenty
metres from them as the minibus stalls. The horsemen surround

it. The Hunt. Fuck. Roll under the hedge and pray my breathing doesn't give me away. To have come so close. The riders bang on its sides and that's all the encouragement the bus needs to fire the ignition and lurch forward, causing the horses to fall back, and it uses this gap to drive through. A few of the riders give chase but they know they're not going to catch it and rein in. The bus is gone and I'm alone. Slide as far as I can into the undergrowth. If they don't see me and think I was on the bus then they'll give up. That makes sense doesn't it? Doesn't it? Can hear them trot up the road until they're practically next to me. That's it, keep on going, keep on going. They stop.

—Did you see that?

—What?

—They were waiting.

—You think?

—They were waiting because one of their number hadn't made it back yet.

—You're right.

—He's still out there.

—Back to the house. We get the hounds and then we hunt for real.

They break into a gallop. Oh fuck. They're getting the hounds, the professionals of the canine world. I lie on my back and look up at the sky. It's time to face the facts Danny, you're gonna get caught. Christ it's cold. Forget about the cold it's excuses we're after. Okay. Imagine a group of angry fat upper class twats looking down from their horses and wanting to hurt you. What's gonna stop them? Nothing's gonna stop them Danny don't waste your time – wait a second! Tell them you work for the government and a terrorist cell is suspected of hiding explosives in graves. Yeah, that could work. Not explosives though, biological weapons. They love that shit. And it's not so stupid because everybody's so paranoid nowadays they probably would buy it and it's about time the bullshit war on terror was used by people like me and not just the fascists to get away with murder. Keep it simple though, don't say you work for the government, just that you happened to be passing and saw something peculiar and decided to investigate. That's not bad Danny, not bad at all. Fuckssake, if the police can shoot a guy for carrying a wooden table leg I can get away with that. Cunts'll probably give me a medal. It'll work. It will. Take a deep breath. Saying something out loud is always a good test to see if it's nonsense. Here goes.

　　–We need to get the police! I think those rascals Al Queda
　　are at it again...
And even with all my hopes trying to alter reality my voice begins to falter and I know they're not going to buy it in a million years.

Another wall. Up and over. Scrape my leg but don't flinch, it's not invulnerability this time it's the opposite, so used to taking cuts and bruises that the pain doesn't have an effect anymore. No idea where I'm going just gotta keep on the move. It's late now, I must have been doing this for hours but it feels longer. No memory beyond today. I never realised the countryside was this big but could easily have been going round in circles so maybe it's not. Almost got caught a couple of times but somehow managed to get out of sight and let the Hunt ride past. Next time they'll get me and I'm almost looking forward to it. Hear the sound of dogs barking and it won't be long. The bag with the skull bumps against me. Why haven't I ditched it?

Don't know, but I'm not leaving it now. Resisted the temptation to talk to it so far but everything's too much and if I don't see a friendly face soon we'll have a proper sit down. The ground under foot suddenly gets harder and then jolts me. I stumble and fall, landing on tarmac. There's a bus stop ahead but it's too late for that now. The dogs are so close they're beginning to whine. Get off the road Danny, don't make it easy for them. I roll to the side and fall into a ditch. I don't move, face down enjoying the clean wetness, and then push myself onto my hands and knees. What's the worst they can do? Kick the shit out of me? I can take that and it's not just bullshit I *can* take that. Fuck em. They're not gonna find me on all fours. It's last stand time. But I don't stand. I freeze. Opposite me, about a metre or so away and equally bedraggled and beaten crouches a fox, its fur torn and teeth bared back in terror and exhaustion. We stare at each other and something passes between us. I reach out towards it but this breaks the spell, scaring the animal, and it bolts onto the road... and straight into the chasing pack. I see everything. The lead hound snaps at the fox's tail, it spins and in its panic doubles back, straight in the direction of the others. They grab it by the throat and then, as other dogs sink their teeth in, rip it to pieces. One thousand nine hundred and one to one. We had a deal didn't we Danny? I hope you've not forgotten. A small group of riders come galloping into view and pull up. The fox's blood has got the dogs into a frenzy and even though I'm only a few metres away they don't pay any heed, the invisible man once again. A young blond guy nods to the others.

—That was the scent they had. Shame.

The riders are barely in their twenties. My age. One of them leans down and scoops up what's left of the fox.

—Anybody want this? he says.

A few of them raise their hands as quickly as they can and it's thrown to the one who reacted first.

—Thanks!

He looks happy. Good for him.

—Let's call it a day. He's not here. He must have been on the bus after all.

It's the blond guy again and the rest grunt in agreement. It takes them a few minutes to round up the dogs and then they're away. I'm free to go. I did it. I escaped.

7

It can't stay here, staring at me from on top of the TV. It's not even my skull. One skull per person, that's how it works. I'll give Shona a call, yeah, get rid of it. She was supposed to be my girlfriend and instead I end up with that bastard on the telly laughing at me.

—Leave a message after the tone.

Answer machine. Good, can't handle talking to her in case she asks about the fox anyway.

—Hi Shona, listen, I say, —I've got the –

What you playing at Danny? Her phone could be bugged. What is the word they always use in gangster films when they're discussing something illegal again?

—I've got the drugs –

Shit.

—I meant thing, not drugs. I've got the thing.

Get out of this conversation now for fuckssake.

—You know what? I don't have anything, not drugs, definitely not drugs. Not even a thing. Nothing. There you go. Talk to you later.

Hang up. That was a disaster. Can't even leave a message on an answer machine without sounding like a reject from *The Wire*.

Sigh. The skull can't stay here. The landlord doesn't let me keep a pet, what the fuck is he going to make of that? Got to drop it off, only thing for it. And that means going outside.

What the hell was I thinking? Sauchiehall Street in the afternoon is like being on the set of a 1970s post-apocalyptic horror film. Got my hand gripped so tightly on the bag with the skull that my whole body feels like it could snap. The grotesqueness of it all. Every third person I pass has got a cast on a broken limb or a scar or a burn or walks with a twisted stoop. If you ever want to make a shit-load of money all you need to do is write a letter to everyone in this city with the words 'I know what you've done' and demand fifty quid because everyone has done something. Everyone has done something and from the looks of it they're on their way to do some more. Faces filled with expressions of hate or fear or blind aggression going about their daily business. Can no one else see this? I dodge an old woman wearing a muddy duvet with a hole cut in the middle so that it's like a poncho but it must have been raining earlier because it's dragging her down and when she looks at me I see what she sees, a creepy young guy gritting his teeth who is so obviously up to no good. Jesus Christ I'm freaking myself out now. Glasgow is a city having a stroke, it just doesn't know it yet, the living part of its brain compensating for the dead, ignoring the bits it can't process or smearing too much makeup over them. Would explain the out-of-context bursts of angry swearing that you can't walk ten metres without hearing and exactly on queue from somewhere to my left –
    —Fuck you ya cunt!
Not directed at me but enough to make me pick up the pace. I pat the bag with the skull.

—It's gonna be okay, I say.

Stop that Danny, don't start a relationship with it. I pass an old guy going through a bin while a group of teenagers watch and laugh, one of them empties a can of coke into the bin as he's still rummaging about, the drink dripping onto his hands. I look at the ground and keep my eyes fixed there, blocking out as much as I can until I'm halfway up Duke Street and close to her flat. Into a side street and I'm almost there. About to cross a road next to a lollipop woman in her sixties, schools must be about to come out, better get a move on, but there's a woman with a toddler waiting as well so I get caught thinking about whether or not I should hold on for the lollipop woman to let me across as I don't want to set a bad example. This is silly Danny. I step off the kerb, holy shit, a car comes from nowhere and I have to jump back onto the pavement beside the lollipop woman, heart pounding. She steps onto the road with her sign.

—You're safe to go now, she says.

Looking at me, not the mother and child. Fucking hell. Outside Shona's building. Security door. No names only numbers, that's just great. I know it's not the ground or top floors so can take those two out, still leaves first and second floor. Buzz one. No answer. Buzz another. And then the first one I buzzed crackles.

—Who's that? a man with a gruff voice says.

Shona stays on her own so it can't be her flat.

—Sorry I didn't mean to buzz you, it was a mistake, I say.

And then the other buzzer I've buzzed clicks.

—What do you want? a second man says.

—I don't want anything you buzzed me, the gruff man says.

—Did I fuck, says the second man.

—You fucking tough enough to say that to my face? says the gruff man.

—You really think I'm gonna let you in now? says the second man.

—You're the one who's outside!

—What the fuck you on? You buzzed me ya cunt!

I clear my throat.

—Sorry, this is all my fault, I say.

—Who the fuck are you? the gruff man says.

—Stay there, I'm coming down and we're gonna sort this out, says the second.

Shit, bang the other buzzers and shout Shona's name but no luck and I can hear a door slam from inside. Take out the skull and try to push it through the letterbox but it's not going to fit and I can't break it into pieces, not after what we've been through. Stick it back in my bag and make a run for it before whatever is about to happen happens. Need to get home and put the skull back on the telly. That's where it belongs. That's where it's going to stay.

At work. Take the key out put the key in the lock. The locker opens. Don't think, do. Get undressed and put the uniform on. Keep my eyes down, stare at the floor, haven't been able to look at myself in the mirror since... Anything could be going on with my hair but it's worth the risk. I feel terrible, worse, I feel nothing. Joe enters, security guard, must be in his sixties. Nice guy but boring, only ever talks about football.

—You're one o' they animal rights protestors ain't you? Anti-fox hunting n'aw that shite?

Where the hell did this come from?

—Who says?

—Joanne.

Fucking poets.

    —They kill chickens. Foxes. You know that don't ye? he says.

Since when did everyone care so much about chickens? If I ignore him he'll stop. He's gotta take the hint. But no.

    —An' another thing, you cannae seriously think that an animal's life is mair important that a human's can ye? What I don't get is how you folk want to save the, whatever, the badger say, when there are people in the world who are in an equally bad, if not worse, position than the sacred badger.

Jesus Fucking Christ. *He only ever talks about football.*

    —What's with the fuckin' badgers man? I say.

Joe steps back.

    —I'm no just talkin' about badgers. I'm using them as an example. I just dinnae understand –

    —I tell you what I don't understand, I don't understand how people like you, who do fuck all to help anybody or anything can take the moral high ground on me. At least I'm doing something.

Yeah, and the last something you did Danny ended in death. Again. But at least it seems to have shut him up. I put my hands in my pockets, they're trembling. Joe sits and sighs. It must be hard being his age and a security guard. Poor bastard.

    —Here's summat though. I've always wondered how it's legal to eat animals but illegal to have sex wi' them. It doesnae seem fair does it? he says.

Since when did it become okay for everyone to take the piss out of me? He chuckles to himself.

    —Ah know you can ha' sex with them after they're deid if

that's yer thing. Of course, you'd probably know a lot more
about that than I do –

—I don't want to make love to them Joe, I say.
Please go away. He claps his hand together and points a fatherly
finger at me.

    —You're a young man Danny. Why don't you forget aw this
rubbish and get yersel' a girlfriend?

    —Fuck you! See if I was a security guard at your age I'd
fuckin' kill myself!

Leave the locker room without looking back and head for the
shop floor. Breathing hard but thank God it's early and practically empty. Even better, my first job is dressing the sugar and
it's like Tetris without the time limit and when it's all stacked
and a solid white brick made up of a hundred smaller ones I'm
relaxed. The anger is replaced by guilt. Shouldn't have said that
to Joe. Time check. 10am. Three hours till lunch. See Mark.

    —Mike's just phoned in sick. You're on your own. Can you
handle it?

I nod and pretend to be disappointed. Need to keep busy. Got
eighteen aisles to keep stocked and neat and tidy all on my lone-
some. That should do it.

Morrison's canteen. I had a table on my own but then Tommy
and Ian came in and sat beside me and I've had to listen to their
bollocks for the last ten minutes.

    —Superman, right, you know how if he sneezes he blows
down doors? Tommy says.

    —I'm with you, says Ian.

    —So what happens when he ejaculates? Wouldn't that be
the equivalent of a gun going off? Danny?

—I don't feel up for this man, I say.

—Poor Lois. I'll tell you something, I wouldn't want to be cleaning the sheets after their wedding night. It'd be like a scene from one of the *Saw* films.

Try to zone out and manage for a bit and then Tommy's slapping me on the top of my head.

—Danny, pay attention, this is serious. *Alien* versus *Predator*, he says.

—What, the film? Ian says.

—No ya fuckin' dick. Not the film. Forget the film, it's pish. Pretend it never happened. I'm talking about in real life. Who do you think would win in a fight?

Ian shrugs and catches my eye.

—Danny? How about it?

Now they're both looking at me and I sense they've made the mistake of thinking that my silence is because I'm contemplating their bullshit conversation as opposed to not giving a toss.

—I dunno, I say.

Check the clock. 1.47pm. Canteen's filling up. Joanne's sitting with Katie at the far end. There are too many people here. And these fucking uniforms. The Morrisons summer outfit designed by Charles Manson. Another ten minutes and my lunch hour's over and then at least I'll be doing something. A month ago I was thinking about jacking this in and going back to Uni but now I prefer to work without a break. Shit.

—You've got to have an opinion though, haven't you? Tommy says.

—Not necessarily, I say.

Tommy shakes his head.

—Dreaming your life away mate, he says.

This motherfucker didn't even vote at the last election and he says this to me?

　—Hold up. Ok. I do have an opinion. *Alien* versus *Predator*, I say. –It's about the battle of the sexes. The *Alien* has essentially got a penis for a face and the *Predator* is a big vagina mouth.

Whoa, said that a bit too loudly and getting a few looks. Tommy's laughing but I'm getting angry.

　—What you laughing about? It's true, I say.

　—You're fuckin' mental mate, Tommy says.

He waves across at Mark who's just entered the canteen.

　—Mark, he says, –did you hear what Danny just said? We were talking about who'd win in a fight between *Alien* and *Predator* and he said his cock looks like the *Alien* and he wants to shag the *Predator*.

　—I don't fancy meeting his girlfriend, Mark says.

　—I don't have a girlfriend, I say.

But it's lost in the laughter thank fuck. Can see some of the women, including Joanne and Katie, looking less than impressed.

　—What a riveting conversation, Joanne says.

Yeah yeah yeah. Can sense that they're whispering about me but I ignore them and stare at my hand as it starts to curl into a fist.

　—So Danny, seeing as how this is your specialist subject, who would win in a fight between Harry Potter and Gandalf? Joanne says.

That didn't take long.

　—Or Luke Skywalker and Captain Kirk?

She and Katie giggle. I'm glad I've brought them closer together. Won't react though, no Sir.

　—Come on, what about God versus the Devil? Joanne says.

Tommy looks to me. Ok then. You asked for it.

—Easy, I say. –Jeffrey Dahmer fantasised about being Satan and when he was killed in prison he was murdered by a guy who, in between cleaning the toilets, believed himself to be Jesus.

Tommy nods, he's always been strong on psychopaths.

—Who's Jeffrey Dahmer? Joanne says.

Tommy guffaws but I hold up my hand.

—He was a serial killer. Drilled holes in young men and had sex with them.

—It's always sex with you, she says.

—What?

—You heard, she says.

And turns her back. Don't fucking turn your back on me. Trembling again but this time I don't try to control it and let it spread.

—Yeah you're right, I say.

She looks at me, unsure, and no please don't but it's too late, I'm standing up and everyone is watching.

—I am obsessed with sex. You know why? You really want to know why?

I'm burning I'm burning and have no idea what I'm saying.

—Cause I'm a cunt hunting fuck fighter, I shout. – That's why. Who wants some?

Silence. Apparently no one.

—So am I by the way, says Tommy.

People start to laugh and I run out of the canteen. Through the shop floor and into the open air. Outside had to get away not even on trolleys but it doesn't matter losing it big style dodging puddles anything that can give a reflection is out of bounds how can I make this stop? There. At the other side of the precinct.

The Golden Arches. A fuckin' McDonalds and on cue I hear a clink underneath my uniform. The handcuffs. Lone gunman time. Clint Eastwood and all that bollocks but it doesn't take much of a switch in perspective for the strong silent type to be a loser with nae mates. Walking mechanically towards it and then push the doors open and I'm inside a McDonald's for the first time since I was seven. What a fucking double-whammy that was, traumatised by the Circus clowns and then brought to Ronald McDonald's death factory to cheer me up. It's surprisingly quiet, an old couple sit on their own at the back while two teenage crew members, one boy, one girl, stand idly at the counter. At least I won't have to queue.

—Can I take your order? the girl says.

Answer her with a twitch and take the handcuffs out, click one cuff on my wrist and the other onto the rail separating us. So far so good. Treble or nothing. They both look at me. A few seconds pass. What the fuck is this? Do I have to do everything?

—Phone head office. Tell them it's started. And while you're at it you'd better get the TV cameras here as well. This is gonna be one of those 'where were you when' situations.

I rattle the handcuffs against the metal rail. It makes a good noise so I do it again. They haven't moved. Come on, let's get this show on the road.

—Have you any idea how evil Mcdonalds is? I say.

—Yeah, you should see how much they pay us, the girl says.

—No. That's not what I mean. I'm talking about the way they exploit animals. And to a lesser extent the environment. That's why I'm here. It stops now.

I rattle the cuffs one last time. The boy finally gets the message and ducks to the back calling someone's name. The girl leans across the counter towards me.

—I'm a vegetarian.

—... That's good.

She seems a nice enough lassie so there's no point taking it out on her and anyway I don't have the chance as another customer enters, a guy in his forties.

–Gonnae move along? he says.

I slide the cuff along the rail to let him in and hear him ordering as what must be the manager appears, a fat guy with glasses. He looks at the cuffs and then at me.

–What do you think you're playing at? he says.

–I'm bringing you down from the inside.

–No you're not. You're making a fool of yourself, that's what you're doing. Look, everybody's laughing at you.

Don't know if that was rhetorical or not but take in the restaurant anyway. The old couple are staring out of the window and the bloke next to me is reading a paper as he waits for his food. Nobody could care less. Call that a score draw. The manager's eyes narrow.

—Isn't this a bit odd? I thought you lot went about in groups. What happened? You get kicked out for patting a dog in the wrong place?

—That's not true! You're way out of your league man. Take that back.

He laughs and disappears. Where the fuck is he going? The girl sidles up to me, looking nervous. She pushes a bun wrapped in greasy paper towards me.

—I got you a veggie burger.

—What?

—Eat it quick. I'll get into trouble if they see you with it.

—I don't want it.

—It's ok, it's vegetarian.

—That's not the point –

She's still trying to force it upon me when the manager returns with a pair of wire cutters. He sees the veggie burger in front of me.

—You'd better be paying for that, he says.

The girl is shitting herself and fuckssake! I pull out a tenner and slam it on the table.

—Happy?

—Give the man his change.

The girl goes to the till and stops.

—You want that as part of a meal deal?

—No I don't want it as part of a fucking meal deal.

She opens the till and I can feel the manager's eyes on me. Where's the press? This is the beginning of an international incident. The start of a revolution. The girl returns with the change. No fucking way.

—I gave you a tenner!

—That's what I was trying to tell you, with fries and a drink it would only have been a pound dearer.

I'm still staring at the change – £3.29 for that? – when the manager comes from behind the counter and cuts the links of the handcuffs. He grabs me by the shoulder and flings me out of the main entrance.

—Piss off. Come back again and I'll kick the shit out of you.

The door closes. Danny, Danny, Danny what have they done to you? Almost see myself reflected in the glass and flinch. Vampires are so lucky. If only I could see nothing. Head across the shopping centre and I suppose I got nothing better to do so it's back to work and oh God this sickness is too much. See

Mark as I enter and clock the time. Five minutes late.

—Your lunch hour finished at two. Where were you? he says.

—Nowhere. What do you want me to do?

He strokes his chin and chuckles to himself.

—Got a new job for you. How does working in the deli sound?

Making a fist so hard it hurts. Is this the time? Is this it?

—Anything else? I say.

You're not gonna lose it Danny, you're not.

—You need to take a good look at yourself in the mirror.

Oh yes you are.

—What d'you say?

—I said I want you to look at yourself at the mirror. The one in the locker room because –

But I've got his head in an arm lock before he can finish and I grab his hair and even though he's bigger than me I'm not letting go and when he falls I fall too and I get kicked in the stomach, by Joe, I think, who's suddenly appeared, and we roll about for a few more seconds and then I let my grip go slack and somebody pulls me from him.

—What you playing at? Joe says.

—He started it.

I point at Mark and what's his problem? He's not got up yet and his hands are covering his face. There's quite a crowd of customers formed mingling with the staff. Ruth, the checkout supervisor, pushes her way to the front.

—How did he start it? she says.

—He told me to look at myself in the mirror, I say.

And I know it's going to make even less sense the more I try to explain it but the blank looks force me to go on.

—It doesn't sound like much but he must have somehow clocked that after the thing with the dogs and the fox at the weekend that... y'know the whole idea of seeing myself wasn't on.

Nobody has a clue what I'm going on about and if this is the last time I see any of these people I better leave them with something good.

—If anybody from McDonalds come looking for me don't give them shit. That place is fuckin' extortionate.

Ruth puts a hand on Mark's shoulder and he looks up. His face is red and he's crying.

—I only told you to look at yourself in the mirror because someone's written 'Joanne fancies Danny' on it, he says.

—That's all.

And hides his face again.

8

Bed. Thank God for bed. Totally under the covers. Cocooned and wombed. Entombed. Bomb sheltered. Don't need to sleep just being here is good enough. Not moving an inch. Never again. Staying put. Why was he crying? I hardly touched him. I didn't want to make him cry. Jesus Christ. What's his problem? I'll give him something to cry about. Probably did him a favour. Crying's good for you anyway, that's what they say. Gets rid of all the shit chemicals. He should thank me. Have your tear ducts surgically altered so that you're crying all the time and everybody's going 'what's the problem?' and you're like 'naw! I feel fantastic!' No wonder people that never cry are such miserable bastards. Try to force myself to shed a tear but it's anxiety I'm feeling not despair and curl tighter underneath the duvet. Too many thoughts on heat-seeking missions. What if someone told Björk that I'd touched her daughter? Where did that come from? But think, what *if* someone *did* tell fucking Björk I'd interfered with her kid? Trying to explain to her that it's not true and I totally respect the way she does her own thing and 'Hit' from when she was in The Sugarcubes is such a good song and isn't it weird that The Wannadies, another Scandinavian group, have a brilliant song called 'Hit' as well and that can't just be coincidence can it? And her just staring right through me.

—You touched my daughter, she'd say. –I'm going to fucking kill you.

—That's a lie Björk. I'll take a lie-detector test to prove it, I've never even been to Iceland –

If she kicked the shit out of that reporter for just saying 'Welcome to Bangkok' what the fuck would she do to me? Should I write her a letter to explain that I've not done anything just in case? And I know it's all bullshit, just my brain being an enemy not a friend but it doesn't stop the panic rising. Feel like I'm gonna throw up. There can't be much oxygen in here that hasn't been recycled a good few times and risk poking my head out for a quick breather. My home. My bed-sit. One room with stove and sink. Toilet. TV. And what's that resting on top? Oh yes. My one and only true friend. The Thirteenth Earl of Talbot. Sweatiness rolling back like the tide, ready to go back under –

Knock.

No.

Knock knock.

No no.

Knockknockknockknock.

Nonononono. And then it stops.

—Danny? You in there? Seb's voice.

Duck under the covers and keep as still as I can.

—Danny? I need your help. I can't set the stall up on my own.

Wait to hear him descending the steps but don't. Poke my head out again. See his fingers appearing through the letterbox, searching for a catch, but finding instead a small plastic hook attached to the door. Excited, the hand tugs and breaks the hook off with a crack, scoring the wood underneath.

—Jesus Christ Seb! What you trying to do? I got a landlord y'know. Why do you think I don't have any pets?

—Oh sorry... But you're there?

I get up and wrap the duvet round me. The hook won't go back without glue and even then it won't hide the damage done to the door.

—Can I come in? he says.

—No, I don't think so.

—What about the stall?

—I'm not doing that sort of thing anymore... I quit.

First time I've said it out loud and it feels good.

—What?

—Yeah, I've changed my mind about trying to help animals. That's it. I'm out.

That wasn't so hard. Getting easier each time. Thought it was gonna be a big deal but it's not, piece of piss.

—Danny, Seb whispers, —is there someone in there with a gun at your head?

—No there isn't someone in here with a gun at my head. I'm just not interested anymore, alright?

—Ok ok. You don't need to shout at me, he says.

I can picture the look on his face, well the top half anyway. Be easy on him Danny. Remember, he looks up to you.

—Sorry Seb. Please, just go.

—I don't get it though. You were always the most into doing stuff.

—I know, but the more I try to do the more damage I do. There were all those dogs at the lab and then at the foxhunt...

—Yeah, what happened? Shona looked like she knew something but I couldn't get anything out of her.

—It was my fault. I got the fox killed.

—You killed the fox?

—No I didn't fuckin' kill it! I'm not gonna go into it, but if it wasn't for me it wouldn't have ran straight into the dogs. I can hear Seb breathing on the other side of the door.

—What you up to then? he says.

—I'm going to bed.

—And then what?

—I'm going to bed for a very long time. Maybe a couple of months.

—Oh. Ok then.

But there's no tread on the stairs. Go Seb, just go.

—Thing is, he says, –I was wanting a word with you myself about some other things as well –

—Night-night, I say.

I shuffle back and collapse on the mattress.

—What do you mean night-night? It's 9am, he says.

But it's faint like he's said it turning away from the door and this time I do hear his footsteps on the stairs. That's it then. My team is no more. Disbanded. The hit squad that was going to change the world and right some wrongs. Norman and the fox. It really did end with a whimper. Fantastic. This need to do something, not content to sit on my arse all day watching TV, thank God it's over. Wednesday Film Club. That's when it started. *Where the people who make the films meet the fans.* Seventeen and thinking

I was hot shit going along to the GFT convinced there'd be tons of French girls there looking to discuss Sartre and I already knew *Nausea* off by heart and even though I didn't really understand it, it didn't seem to matter. But I arrived late and the film had already started and then in the bar where we were all supposed to meet afterwards to discuss what we'd seen there were only two women and everybody was older than me and out of nervousness when the director asked for any questions about the beginning I blurted out –

— My bus was late, what happened in the first fifteen minutes?

And at the start thinking it was good to get such a big laugh but then realising that these people, this group, were getting such a kick out of my embarrassment that it could only be coming from a bad place. Fuckin' GFT. Saw *Amelie* there and then tried that thing of watching other people in the cinema when they don't realise they're being watched at the Forge Parkhead during one of the *Batman* films and thinking how cool and sophisticated I was and then seeing that guy having a dump in the drinks holder beside his seat. Totally ruined any chance I had of ever enjoying foreign films cause it's hardwired in my brain, somebody mentions French cinema and all I see is a silhouette straining silently and it plopping out. Yep. Fuck all groups. Better off without them. Duvet over the head then over and out.

— Danny!

Hear it but don't react. How much time has passed? A day, a week, a month? Check the clock. An hour and a half. Bloody hell.

— Danny! Get up man, I need you, this is serious.

Seb again. Can I pretend not to be in? Look over and see the mark on the door where he tore the hook off. If I don't answer the cunt'll trash the flat.

—Jesus Christ Seb. We've already had this conversation. Leave me alone.

Leave me alone. Oh no. I really said that. I'm becoming a teenager again. Would explain the morbid commitment to masturbation.

—Danny, it's Paul, he's in trouble. Open up, he says.

—What you so concerned about Paul for? Last I heard you punched him in the face.

—I know I but this is different. Let me in.

Sigh and get up. Unlock the door. Seb looks flushed and for once without a scarf covering half his face. How young he looks. Must be living in the commune, fresh air n' that but still, any time you see them on the telly they look manky.

—Make it quick, I say.

—Went round to Paul's to see if he wanted to help me set up the stall, y'know, to make up for being such a prick, he says. –But there was no answer and I was just about to leave when I heard a scream.

—Why did you go round to his anyway? You know he's only doing this to help him pull?

—Yeah, that's why I punched him, but nobody else was gonna help and you need two to carry all the gear.

Ok. So that means…

—You went round to Shona's? I say.

—Yeah. Danny, put some clothes on, we should hurry.

And he's in my room and flinging clothes at me which I start to put on automatically.

—What did she say then?

—She told me to piss off.

Thinking about this as I pull a t-shirt on when we both glance at the TV at the same time. The skull. Fair play to Seb, he looks away and pretends he didn't see it.

—You ready?

I nod and if he hadn't seen the skull maybe I would have stayed but now it seems good to leave and I don't know whether it's being with someone or the fact that we're going to help another human being but going outside doesn't have the same terror it did moments ago. Seb's in front of me as we hit the street and opens the door to a mini that's practically brand new.

—Where did you get this?

He looks embarrassed.

—Oh. I borrowed it.

He's got a real thieving problem this one.

—If we get stopped you told me it was yours right?

He nods and we're in. Stare out of the window. This isn't part of the plan. Can see Seb's nervous and not in the mood for talking, concentrating on driving and dodging the police. That's all I need, a joy ride. There's a copy of *The Herald* on the back seat and I take a look and the first story I see is about a sixty-year-old woman in Germany who had an epileptic fit and her dog, a bull terrier, attacked and chewed her face off. I did not need this. The dog was hers. It was her pet. What happened to getting help from the neighbours with the old double-bark routine? Lassie's nemesis. Bad Lassie. I groan and fling the paper away but it's lodged in my head and I can't get rid of it. From Bad Lassie it's only a small step to Evil Guidedog. An innocent looking golden retriever by day but when it's alone with its master it pisses in the food, barks in the middle of

the night to trick him into thinking it's the morning, bites his
hand while crossing a busy road and fucks off leaving him to
get knocked down by a lorry. Forget it Danny, Evil Guidedogs
don't exist, yet my brain's got a life of its own and even when
I'm telling myself to move on I see the Evil Guidedog sneaking
into an antiques shop, stealing a stuffed animal and putting
it in its bed so in the morning its blind owner will think his
best friend and helper has died in his sleep. I pick up the paper
again and manage to use the death of an American soldier as a
distraction. Panic passed and we're slowing down and parking
outside Paul's. Get out and up the stairs to the second floor. Seb
looks at me to take the lead but I shrug and he knocks. There's
no answer.

   —He just wants to be left alone, I say. —Maybe you're the
   one with problem?
Seb shakes his head.

   —Paul! he shouts. —It's me and Danny. We're here to help.
Nothing and I'm in the process of turning away when we hear
a wail. And then glass smashing. And another wail.

   —Paul? Are you ok in there? I say.
There's a mad laugh and a bit of the dread that's been resting on
me is transferred to what's going on beyond the door.

   —Fuck it.
I step back and boot it, the door doesn't go first time but Seb
joins in and then we're both knocking lumps out of it. Quite
good fun actually. The wood splinters and the door opens at
an angle, the bottom hinge off. I go in. Paul's flat is even more
of a mess than I remember, a computer with a burnt monitor
lying against the floor and empty fast food containers (fucking
KFCs and Burger Kings aplenty, the bastard), then it's through

the hall to where I can hear sobbing. The toilet lies before us. Seb nudges me. I really don't want to be doing this but I push the door open anyway. Paul is on the floor staring at himself in a shard of what was recently the bathroom cabinet mirror. Tiny bits of glass form a little glinting semi-circle round the toilet bowl but the effect is anything but magical. There's blood and lots of it and it's coming from his face, if the hole was a vagina before it's now the vagina of an alien with serious gynaecological problems. The place stinks of TCP and even worse I can see a few clots of red cotton wool soaked in disinfectant that he must have used on his face. Oh God save us, *the sting*. Seb's behind me and even more freaked out than I am and when Paul turns to us I realise that he isn't *looking* at the shard in his hand, he's got it poised above his wrist.

—A'right? I say.

Paul doesn't answer and just sobs some more.

—How are things?

He looks up at me, madness in his eyes.

—I'm gonna slit my wrists. Why don't you just fuck off?

I stand there for a moment not moving before I get on the floor with him and trying not to feel uncomfortable as I put an arm around his shoulder. He pushes me off but when Seb joins us the push turns to a pull and we're all tight together.

—It's gonna be ok, Seb says.

—No it's not, he says.

He spits and there's saliva in the blood.

—Did Danny tell you about my low self-esteem?

Seb looks at me and I shrug. Paul points at the hole in his cheek,

—Trust me, he says, —this is the worst possible thing that could happen to someone who's already got low self-esteem.

I mean, what bird's gonna look at me now?

—That'll heal in a couple of weeks and then you'll be right as rain, Seb says.

That thing's never gonna heal. Is Simon Weston getting better? Paul sniffs and wipes a tear away. He looks me in the eye.

—What do you think Danny?

—Oh aye. Just you wait and see. Before you know it the women will be lining up.

He takes a deep breath, calming down, and tries to smile.

—That's true. I am great with the ladies, amn't I?

For fuckssake his last serious relationship was stalking a stripper.

—Oh yeah, you're the man when it comes to the opposite sex, Seb says.

—Do you know why?

—… Not really, I say, –but that can probably wait –

—Because I'm a gigolo.

He pronounces it 'giggle-o'.

—I laugh women into bed.

Me and Seb laugh and that's what Paul needed because he starts chuckling himself, though a bit too much because some fluid squirts from his face causing him to grimace.

—We should get you an elastoplast, Seb says.

—Where you gonna find one that size? I say.

Seb looks at me like I'm being unhelpful but unless the invisible man's head bandage counts as an elastoplast we got a problem.

—Ok. Forget about the elastoplast, Seb says. –But you know what? We need to get you out of this place and back into the real world, ain't that right Danny?

Don't like the sound of where this is going but I nod anyway.

—We were just on our way to set the stall up, Seb says.
I shake my head at him but he gives me his puppy dog eyes and
fuckin' hell I'm not doing this anymore but I can see why he
wants to get Paul out of here. Depression takes second place to
suicide but part of me thinks he's just attention seeking and if
there's anyone who's got a right to be suicidal it's me.

—I can't go out looking like this, Paul says.

—You'll stay here by yourself?

—Yeah.

Seb gives a little sigh. Jesus Christ.

—I don't think that's such a good idea, I say. –You should
come along.

He shakes his head.

—I can't.

—I know how you feel! Seb says. –I've had a big spot on
my face before and not wanted anyone to see me, but every
single time that's happened I've gone out and in the end
really enjoyed myself!

Paul points at the hole in his face.

—This isn't a spot Seb.

—Yeah, we understand, I say. –But the last thing you need
right now is to be on your own. You know that, don't you?

Paul doesn't react. Seb punches him on the shoulder.

—This'll be fun.

This is terrible. Oh God this is terrible. I'm not supposed to be
here. I'm supposed to be in bed having a breakdown but Paul
has beaten me to it. His suicidal urge didn't last long cause
now he's high as a kite running after people to get them to give
donations, two collecting cans hanging from his shoulders and

another in his hands. When he crashes there's gonna be trouble.
I'm behind the stall with Seb, watching. This is all his fault.
Bastard.

   —How you feeling? Seb shouts.

Paul turns and gives a thumbs up, leaking a smile at us.

   —Great! he says.

Then runs after an old woman rattling his cans and out of fear
she coughs up some money. Seb looks at me, worried, but I
don't respond. Paul slams a collecting tin on the table.

   —Another full one. Youse guys were right, this is far better
   than being on my own. It's good to be good.

Then he's off again lurching after a woman in a wheelchair.

   —This doesn't change anything, I say.

   —What?

   —This, what we're doing, I'm only here cause Paul was
   gonna top himself. I won't be doing it again.

Seb takes it in and purses his lips.

   —Danny, I want to talk to you about something...

He pauses and I whistle, don't even know what tune. Fuckin'
hell, it's the *Cheeky Girls* song. Enough is enough.

   —I'm off.

I start walking, the thought of peace and quiet and a new wank
record burning inside me. Seb blocks the way.

   —I need to tell you –

I close my eyes and break into a run, accidentally catching my
foot on the stall and stumbling to a fall. Don't want to open my
eyes ever again but it's not my decision and when I land on the
concrete I see Seb standing over me with his arms outstretched
trying to help me up. I take his hand and manage to keep one
eye closed, Christ I hope he doesn't think I'm winking at him,

and once I'm up he's still trying to talk to me but it's too late for
that and I'm away. I'm away.

9

I know what I have to do but I don't want to do it. Not much time left. I'll have a cup of coffee and then go. Yeah. Switch the kettle on. Put the coffee in and then the milk so it's all ready to roll. As soon as the water boils there'll be no time wasted. Ok. It's 8pm. Morrisons closes at 9pm. I'm owed what I'm owed. No matter how painfully it finished I did my bit and deserve my fair share. Two weeks work, that's almost £500. I need that money. And so it's time to face the music. Jesus, this kettle's taking its time. I could always go tomorrow during the day. Why should I feel embarrassed about seeing Mark and Joe and Katie and Joanne and all the rest of them? Why go at night when it's people I don't know quite as well and who weren't working that day? It's decided then, I'm definitely going tonight. After the coffee. Probably be Margaret on. Should be straightforward, she'll want to get rid of me as quickly as I want to leave. Now then, what about this coffee? Water still boiling, could have gone and switched the TV on or got a book but there's no point now. Waiting for the kettle to boil. That shit adds up. All the important things you could do in the time wasted waiting for stuff, put buses at the top of the list. Or the things that happen to others while you're doing nothing. People you know, people you love, will be dying while you're killing time at some point in your life. Washing dishes or watching daytime TV or just staring into space. During one of those bits of meaningless existence somebody close to you will be breathing their last. Is this the *This Morning* when your gran died? Or the wank interrupted phonecall you got to tell you that there's been a crash and you've got to go straight to the hospital to identify the bodies? The episode of *Coronation Street* when your brother got cancer? There's a plot twist you didn't see coming and they say the storylines are getting predictable. Maybe getting killed in an aeroplane disaster, or hit by a stray meteorite, or savaged by a wild squirrel is a million or even millions to one, but put them all together and the fact is it's odds on that something terrible will happen to you at some point in your life and if by some fluke you dodge it you can guarantee that the ones closest to you will get double. Put my hand on the side of the kettle to get a heat. It's cold. Eh? Pour some water from the kettle into the sink and touch it. It's tepid at best. Bloody kettle's broke, must be the element. Fucking waste of time. Gotta leave now. Step towards the door. See the skull. Could do with the support and put in my bag. Don't want to think where this is going but it's not really weird it's just my security blanket is a human skull. Perfectly normal.

8.50pm. Skirt round the McDonalds. No need for any sequels. Okay, I've left it as late as I can, after 9pm it's nightshift and I can forget about talking to a manager that can help. Should be dead by now, hardly any customers and the staff getting ready to leave. Car park traversed. Not seen anyone I know yet that's good. Screw being scared. Be a man Danny. Automatic doors open and I'm in. As I thought, no one about, only a single checkout still open, a girl I've never seen before, young and wearing too much make-up. I head her way. My God, she really has gone overboard on the cosmetic front.

—Where's the manager? I say.

—I've not done anything, she says.

—What?

—I've not done anything.

Jesus Christ. But the anger flashes and dies, the wee lassie must only be sixteen and looks terrified.

—No I'm not complaining, I say. –I work here, I mean I used to work here.

She stares at me. What's her problem?

—Are you Danny?

—Yeah. How do you know my name?

But she just continues to stare at me. And doesn't say anything.

—It's your turn to talk, I say.

—What?

—You asked me a question, I answered, now it's your turn.

She makes a face like I'm the mental one here.

—It's ok, I'll find the manager on my own. Thanks a lot. And by the way, what's with the war paint love? This is Morrisons not a Mexican whorehouse.

Walk past her and feel good. That's what I needed, a bit of aggro to pump myself up, and ok, she was a sixteen year-old girl but in this world you gotta take any victories you can. The manager on duty must be about somewhere and I start heading up the aisles but can't see anyone, could always go to the back, check the canteen or the office on the second floor, but after the days in bed I'm knackered and why do I have to go looking for them when they're the ones that owe me money? Pass a girl I

vaguely know stacking shelves, she smiles at me with lips bright
red, a smudge of lipstick on her teeth. They're all going for it
tonight. Quicken my step as I pass the fresh meat section and
then stop. There it is before me. Should I? No, yeah, go on, the
business with the checkout girl has given me a bit of fire so fuck
it. I pick up the store announcement phone attached to the wall.
Let them come to me. Clear my throat and nod at the woman
behind the fish counter. Plastered foundation under neon lights
does not go. Somebody should tell her. Tell them.

— Could the manager on duty please...

Check the woman again. Why is she so made-up? Fuck no, hear
a big laugh from the front of the store, a load of people in high
spirits have just entered. There's a clock at the end of the store
and underneath the date. The date. Shit. This is the works night
out. This is the fuckin' works night out. Everybody's gonna be
here. That's why the women look like they do, those in tonight
will be going straight out after their shift. The voices are getting
louder and I can distinguish Mark and Joanne's laugh amongst
the others. Something's drowning them out and though at first it's
a relief not to hear the laughter, the new sound is disquieting, like
what you'd expect at a sex criminals convention. Heavy breathing. Exceptionally loud heavy breathing. And that's when they
come round the corner. Mark at the front of a bunch of about
ten of my ex-colleagues with a big grin on his face and wearing
one of those shiny petroleum shirts that were in fashion years ago
and even then weren't really. Seeing me he stops smiling. Oh God
I hope he doesn't cry again. I couldn't take it.

— You're frightening the customers, he says. *—I am your
father Luke!*

Jesus fucking Christ what the fuck is that supposed to mean?

No. It's me. I'm still on the phone. Exhaling my horror in a way that sounds even more terrible externally than internally. I've been giving the whole store a dirty phonecall.

    —Right. Got you, I say. –Darth Vader. Good one.

I put the phone down. Feel a sweat coming on.

    —Who you looking for? Mark says.

    —Whoever's on. The manager, y'know, to sort out my pay after the… well, you know, you were there.

    —I can do that, he says.

    —Naw it's alright. I'll sort it out with whoever's on.

    —I'm on, kinda, you're never off working for these bastards.

He grins and rolls his eyes. No idea what he's playing at. He should hate me not try to be my friend.

    —No, seriously, I say. –It's alright –

    —I want to do it –

    —No –

    —It'll take me two minutes, have you got your timesheet?

    —Give it up Mark, it's not happening. I know your game.

He finally gets the message and shrugs.

    —I just wanted to help.

And drops his eyes and if he starts crying I really will give him something to fucking cry about. Or possibly join in.

    —You coming then? Joanne says.

    —Eh?

    —On the night out.

    —I don't think so –

    —Go on –

    —Come on Danny –

    —Wouldn't be the same without you –

A few others join in. People I don't even know but already

a little drunk and into the whole encouraging someone who doesn't want to do something into doing it.

—I'd love to but I don't work here anymore, I say. —The night out is only for people that actually, y'know, work here. They've always been pretty strict about it.

—That's bullshit, says an aggressive young guy I've never seen before. —That's a fuckin' disgrace.

A few grunts from the other. What does it matter to them if I go or not?

—How about it Mark? Joanne says, —You're management.

No no no no no.

—Of course he can come, Mark says, —I was just gonna say.

This isn't so bad. Don't know what I was frightened about. Being in a pub with a group of people you work with, used to work with, is fine. And if not actual fun at least it's killing time. I'm getting drunk but a good drunk which is a surprise. Got my hand glued to the handle of the bag. The skull. If it were to fall out in some sort of classic sitcom type way it wouldn't be funny at all. I've ended up with the young thug that was so desperate for me to come out and his mate, a prick who must be new like him. Joanne and Mark and the rest of them are at the other side of the bar. So far not much talking just speed drinking, which suits me.

—Danny, same again mate? says Thug.

—Cheers.

—Make mine a double vodka this time, says Prick.

—Check it out. Big man wi' his doubles. Fuckin' poof. Why not trebles? Whaddaya say Danny?

Know what's expected of me and can't bear the look on their faces if I let them down. They're both so desperate to have a good time, so committed to doing everything that they're supposed to do being young, stupid and proud of it that there's an honesty about them that is almost heroic. Get the feeling that going to a strip club at the end of the night when they're totally pissed and there only to be ripped off isn't so much a choice as it is a moral obligation. They're smiling at me, waiting for the line, but it's their vulnerability that's showing and like everybody else they're probably only one hurtful insight away from bursting into tears.

—Trebles? Didn't realise I was drinking with girls. Fucking quadruples. Get them in, I say.

This gets a whoop from them both and Thug punches my shoulder.

—Ok old timer. Let's see if you can handle a night out with the *outlaws*.

On cue Thug and Prick put their hands inside their jeans as if to scratch their arses and then do a fast draw with their thumb and forefinger, pushing their digits towards each other's nose trying to make the other smell.

—Fuckin' love that don't you?

—Aw! You've got a sweaty bum.

—It's not sweat –

—Just get the drinks in ya dirty bastard!

They giggle and Thug leaves, pushing his way to the front of the bar and I'm left with Prick. Small, eighteen or nineteen years old maybe. He looks at me and smiles, a little creepy crease of his face. Find myself missing Thug.

—What's got ten tits and stinks? he says.

—I dunno.

—The bin in a breast cancer ward.

He laughs then stops.

—I can make that joke cause that's how my mum died.

—Oh.

—Cancer. Not of the tits though.

—Right.

—So it's not like I'm taking the piss. For me it's a sign of respect.

—Yeah.

—Thanks for not laughing by the way.

Prick stares at the floor, dropping his empty glass that he then lazily kicks to hit off the ankle of a girl wearing a short skirt and boots. Glance over and see Mark talking with a woman. She's actually laughing at what he's saying but I can sense that it's false and she's just waiting for the chance to leave. Feel another wave of guilt about making him cry. Will have to apologise properly, do it after a few more drinks. Prick's greetin' but that's got nothing to do with me so ignore it. Gotta get more alcohol in me and start moving towards the bar, banging into Thug on his way back carrying three Bacardi Breezers.

—What the fuck is this shit?

—They don't sell quadruples, not even trebles. Doesnae matter anyway, listen.

He grabs my hand and forces a sweaty pill into my palm.

—Met a pal who got us sorted. You'll waste it if you get too drunk so calm down the boozing for a bit. It was a tenner each so let's see it.

Not sure I want it but hand him the money anyway. Thug clocks Prick who's still crying and has to shout at him to be heard above the music that's suddenly gone up a notch or two.

—What's the matter? Is it yer maw's cancer? Is it yer maw's cancer again?

That's enough for me and I put the pill in my mouth and only then as I'm swallowing realise that the hand he was holding it in was fingering his arse only moments before.

Nothing. Fuckin' nothing. Fuckin' bullshit fuckin' dud. That's a tenner wasted on the gear and another ten getting into this fuckin' club and if I stay I'll need to get a lot more booze in which will probably be at least £3.50 a drink, at least. Bastards. I didn't even want to come out tonight and it's cost me a fortune. Thug. Thug's fault. Him and his cunt mate. Probably knew it was a dud all along. Thug and Prick having a good laugh cause they sold me a smartie for a ten spot. He's here somewhere and fuck it but I'm getting my money back. Pass the cloakroom and the toilets to the dance floor. See him standing at the side with a few of young guys from work, Joanne and Katie and Mark and the rest in a separate group next to them. Fuckin' left sock's slid under my heel as well and it only happens in these shoes why the fuck is that? Kneel down to pull it back up and the exit is straight ahead of me but no fucking way. I'm getting my money back and if he wants trouble he's got it. Cunt sold me a fuckin' dud. Something needs to be done. Lift an empty bottle that's lying on a table and head his way. This fucker is paying and I don't care how many mates he's got.
   —Danny! You alright? Thug says.
   —Naw I'm not ya fuckin' arsehole.
Christ he's got good skin, never noticed it in the pub.
   —What's the problem?
   —You're the fuckin' problem pal.
New song comes on and I know it, it's a classic. *Mojo. Lady.* Fuck me but that's good.

—What did I do? he says.

Nod my head to the beat and my hand makes waves with the sound.

—You sold me a fuckin' dud.

He looks at me blankly for a second then points at my hand and I see it doing a ski jump all on its own and he smiles and I smile and we both start laughing and I give him a hug and holy shit this is gonna be an absolutely fucking brilliant night I just know it. Another rush almost knocks me off my feet and this must be pretty strong stuff and I'm such an arsehole for even thinking that he'd scammed me and I start trying to tell him but he just nods like it's no big deal and not to worry about it and he's right. We're cool. All of us. Sense someone at my shoulder and turn. It's Joanne.

—You ok? she says.

—Fuckin' brilliant.

Need to hit the dance floor but it's too early and completely dead.

—Want to go somewhere a bit quieter to talk?

—Em...

See her face shift and feel the rejection more acutely than she does.

—Sure. Outside the bogs?

She leads me out into the brighter walkway between the different rooms. Too fucking bright. Can still hear the music and can't help but move.

—Glad you came? she says.

—Yeah. Thanks. If it wasn't for you I wouldn't be here.

She smiles and doesn't say anything. I trace my tongue over my teeth, my mouth suddenly dry. Notice a glass of something in her hand and reach for it.

—Can I have a taste? I say.

—Sure. Be careful though. This drink will get you laid.

I try not to think about what she's just said and raise the glass to my lips.

—One sip and you're fucked, she says.

And take a drink. FUCK.

—It's straight vodka. Katie smuggled a half bottle in, I'm just holding it for her.

That's brilliant, my mouth isn't just dry anymore it's fucking on fire. Got to get back in there where it's dark and the people are nice.

—Want to dance?

—No. I don't really like this music.

I nod but I'm not agreeing with her.

—Do you like me? she says.

—Yeah. Course I do.

—Good. I like you too.

Oh Christ. She's bringing me down. The idea of a seventeen-year-old lassie trying to get off with me or even worse, getting really drunk and following me about for the rest of the night is terrifying.

—I think we're quite similar really, except I have friends, she says.

—Eh?

—I mean we're both loners but I have friends as well.

She gives me a little smile and holds my hand and even though the skin feels great I pull away.

—I have friends too. What about Thug and Prick?

—Who?

—Thug and Prick. Especially Thug. I don't know their real names –

Right on cue Thug passes us on his way to the toilet.

—Tell her. Are we mates or what?

—As of tonight he's one of the outlaws.

Thug sticks his hand down his trousers but I shake my head
and he pulls it back out again and glides off down the corridor.
I turn to Joanne, vindicated.

—See, I say.

But I almost fall due to another rush and have to lean against
the wall to steady myself.

—What's wrong? Are you drunk? she says.

—Not drunk.

—Is it drugs? she says.

For some reason she looks shocked but I smile to put her at ease.
Fuck me but this is really good stuff.

—Stay here, she says. —I'll get a bouncer to phone an
    ambulance.

She's moving before I can react and there's a huge bald door-
man only seconds away. Shit. Fuckin' run back to the dance
floor and at least there's a couple of people on it and thank
fuck they're on E as well because they smile when I join them
and there's none of the bullshit when people are drunk. Joanne
enters with the bouncer and they come towards me but I turn
away and when she touches my shoulder I look surprised like I
don't know her and the bouncer leaves without saying a word.
Joanne stays and tries to dance but looks hurt and confused and
I'm not intentionally ignoring her anymore but I get really into
the music and close my eyes and when I open them again the
dance floor is packed but she's gone.

Being alive is great. I'm feeling pretty loved up and nobody's come close to annoying me yet, not even the really pissed guy who's staggering about the dance floor banging into everyone and so obviously looking for a fight. The DJ, a wee fat guy, is a total God and everyone looks so eerily healthy we could be movie stars at the Oscars, except instead of Billy Crystal hosting it's William Shatner. As in fucking awesome. I get locked onto a light that comes up every twentieth beat and put my hands up each time it blinks. Smooth. The light changes frequency and I continue to put my hands up at every flash, which is now four times a second, like a fucking human humming bird beating its wings but manage to stop before I think anyone notices. Not smooth. Relax Danny. And I get back into the groove, chilled out. See Mark dance close beside me, the lassie he was with must have told him to beat it. Didn't take long, poor bastard. I place an arm on his shoulder.

—Sorry Mark.

—What? he says.

—Sorry!

He shakes his head, pointing at his ears, and I know I should leave it but I gotta get this off my chest and although he puts up a bit of a fight I manage to drag him off the dance floor where the music is ever so slightly less thumping. He keeps glancing away like he's looking for someone else.

—I want to talk to you Mark, I say.

He's still not meeting my eyes so I put an arm around his neck, just to get his attention.

—I'm sorry.

He finally gets it and gives me a blank look.

—For what?

The girl I saw him talking to earlier appears and hands him a drink but I can't let anything distract me, I'll never get this chance again.

—For what happened in the store, I shout.

The girl's leaning over as well, listening.

—I didn't mean to make you cry, I'm sorry man.

I tap him on the arm, smile at the lassie and head back to the dance floor.

Should have called it a night after the club, was still dancing when the lights came on and got a shock even though it's always the same. The reduced to clear section. Only the drunk and desperate for a snog remain. And just like the reduced to clear in Morrisons, chances are if you pick anything up you'll be sick in the morning. But I was still feeling great and it was too hard to leave it all behind so here I am, at a party in a flat owned by the brother of one of Thug's mates, hoping that the line of speed Thug gave me is going to do the trick but wishing it was more E. Being alive doesn't feel so great anymore, not after everything, and if the E was a dam the speed's a goddamn dambuster. Got myself base camped in the kitchen and haven't talked to anyone since I arrived. I'm a fucking tarantula sitting on a washing machine waiting to pounce. I've fought the need to speak for so long that it's too much and even though I got no idea who this is, just some poor sod who's getting a beer from the fridge, it all comes gushing out in a torrent –

—Hi I'm Danny. Anyway, you know what I'm talking about don't you? The abyss man, the fucking hole where life ends but you keep on existing, teetering on the edge for infinity reliving all the bad stuff you've ever seen or done –

It's because I'm in the kitchen, it's the fuckin' kitchen's fault, not mine, like the whole Stephen King *Shining/Salem's Lot* thing about evil places drawing evil, it's the same with kitchens and depressing bullshit at four in the morning.

    —and I'm telling you man I've seen some things that I don't want to see again, seriously.

The guy looks at me. He's late teens and I'm egging him on with my eyes praying he knows what I'm talking about. He opens the can of beer and takes a sip. How can he possibly have a clue what it's like?

    —Mate I'm here for you, he says. —You got stuff you need to get off your chest, go for it. We're all in this boat together. You'd do the same for me.

God bless this motherfucker. He leans against the work top like he knows this is gonna take some time and he'd better get comfy. He's just gonna let me talk. The guy's a goddamn saint.

    —This abyss you're talking about. What about it? he says.

    —The abyss. Right. Falling without end. You're dead but you're not dead cause you're aware that you're dead which means you can't be. Dread, y'know? Fucking dread.

Can hear the sound of talking from the hall but don't let it distract me. I've got my karmic hostage and I'm not releasing him until my demands are met.

    —There's no heaven there's no hell, only the abyss. The fucking abyss man, get me? This huge fucking hole in the ground, the biggest hole in the planet.

A snort. It's the bloke who owns the flat, didn't even hear him come in. He's nodding.

    —Been there. Fucking brilliant, he says.

    —Eh?

—The big fucking hole in the ground, he says. —Got
married overlooking it.

Jesus fucking Christ, sick lumps in my throat.

—What you talking about? You can't get fucking married
there.

—Yeah you can. We did the whole thing, Las Vegas, Los
Angeles then got married at the Grand Canyon. Talk about
a big fucking hole in the ground. I'm Bob by the way.

He extends his hand which I take automatically. The kid who
was gonna listen to me, who was gonna fuckin' *listen* to me
squeezes past him and heads out the door. Bob stays.

—You been? To the Grand Canyon?

I shake my head.

—Stay here. I got some pics, marriage ones as well. Don't
go anywhere.

He leaves. I spew in the sink but it's frothy and isn't hard to
get rid of. Bob will be back soon with his camera. The abyss.
Nothing can save me. The kitchen door opens, expecting Bob but
it's Joanne. She's my only chance.

—Please, I say. —Take me home.

In a taxi and she's dealing with the driver. Thank God for
Joanne, I'll remember this. I was bad to her earlier, will make
up for it in the future.

—I really appreciate it, I say. —The guy in there was about
to show me his wedding pictures. You're a superhero. They
should make a statue of you.

She laughs. Great girl.

—I don't usually do this, she says.

—Do what?

—Take people back to my place.

Fuck. I thought she was taking me home, to my home, not hers, not hers. And then she's sitting beside me as the taxi drives off and her mouth is moving towards mine and it does cross my mind to pull away but I can't, it would be too mean, so we kiss and I've just been sick but at least I rinsed my mouth and while this is going through my mind her hands are all over me, inside my top, she's even squeezing one of my nipples, bloody hell, when did girls start doing that? She puts my hand on her left tit and I just leave it there because it'd be rude to take it off. The hand that was just fiddling for Radio 4 on my nipple has moved down to the top of my jeans and thank fuck they're a size too small but she's not having any of it and her nails scratch as they force their way in and I can't help but give a little scream.

—Sorry, she says.

But at least we've stopped kissing and so I smile and open my mouth to change the subject and then she's back, knocking my head against the side window, kissing me like she really wants to. Either she's incredibly into me, in a Romeo and Juliet kinda way, or a complete and utter nympho. One thing's for sure, I'm fucked. Some more wrestling goes on which I am about lose on a submission when the taxi stops somewhere in the South Side. Hand over some cash and get out. Nice houses. Very nice houses. Oh thank fuck. Of course, that's why she was going for it in the taxi.

—You live with your parents, I say.

And try not to let the relief in my voice show.

—Yeah, she says.

—We don't want to wake them and it is getting late so maybe it's best if I –

Her eyes narrow.

—What is this? she says.

—Nothing –

—You want to leave just cause we're not going to have sex?

—No, no, it's not that, honestly –

—You can still come in for a chat, can't you? she says.

—Yeah sure. Love to.

Up some steps and she opens the door to a beautiful old Victorian town house. Trying to be quiet but every floorboard squeaks and I bet her dad is a judge or something and I'll end up doing twenty years for this. Into the living room, a leather couch and two enormous armchairs. Manage to make it to a chair without it seeming like I was dodging the couch. Got my bag with the skull at my feet, can't forget that no matter what else happens. Check the clock on the wall, quarter to five. This can't last long.

—I'm sorry about what happened in the club, I say.

—You didn't look well, she says. —I was worried about you.

I nod. I've apologised. Nothing else for me to do here.

—I feel like we've really clicked, she says.

—So when do your parents usually get up? I say.

—Don't worry about them, she says. —Let's play a game.

—I didn't know you had an Xbox –

—No, a different sort of game. Five questions.

—Like Trivial Pursuit?

—Not really. Question number one. What are you most proud of?

A long pause. This is harder than Trivial Pursuit. Is there anything I'm proud of?

—I can hold my breath for over a minute, I say.

—My turn, she says, –I can speak three languages.

—Really?

She drops her head shyly.

   —It's no big deal, it's not like holding my breath for over a
   minute, she says.

Is she taking the piss? Can't tell, she may just be feeling sorry
for me, which is worse.

   —What's the next question? I say.

   —Tell me something you've never told anyone?

   —You go first, I say.

She shakes her head.

   —I can't.

Remember Danny, she's only seventeen. Time for you to show
your maturity.

   —I'll go then. I used to steal stuff from the shop. Don't
   know why, crap like staplers and pens. Didn't even use
   them. See, we've all got things we're embarrassed about.

She looks me in the eye.

   —I give ten percent of my earnings to charity, she says.

Fucking hell she must be taking the piss now! Don't let her get
to you Danny, don't.

   —Next question, I say, —And for this one, to stop any cheating, we'll both write our answers down on a piece of paper
   at the same time.

She takes a pad from the coffee table and tears off a page and
hands it to me, keeping the rest for herself. I get a couple of
pens from my bag, fuck, almost let the skull out there, and hand
her one.

   —Is this stolen? she says.

   —Next fucking question, I say.

   —Don't be like that –

—I'm sorry, I say. —But what is the next question?

—What is your biggest flaw? she says.

Okay, got this one covered. We both scribble down our answers.

—Shall I read it out then? she says.

—No, I'll read yours and you can read mine.

She hands me the piece of paper.

—*I don't think anyone has flaws, the sting of a nettle isn't a flaw of nature, in its unique way it's as beautiful as the most colourful butterfly.*

For fuckssake. Joanne looks down at my answer.

—... Do you want me to... ?

—Just read the bloody thing, I say.

—*I sometimes get out of buying my round by pretending I need to catch a bus*, she says.

And that's not even true, it's been years since I've done it and they were all a bunch of pricks anyway, who paid for all the crisps? Who paid for all the fucking crisps? Did they reimburse me for those? Did they fuck.

—I'll ask the questions from now on, I say —What star sign are you?

—Libra.

—Ha! I shout, —I think we're all fucking stars!

Breathing hard and why am I letting myself get worked up? but at least she starts laughing and I join in, as if I've been joking about the whole thing from the get go. Check the clock again, it's almost five, her neo-con parents must be getting up soon to exploit some workers.

—Let's play another game, she says.

—Good idea, but look at the time –

—Truth or dare, she says.

Listen, it's five o'clock in the morning, what about your mum and dad?

I grab my bag and get to my feet, already backing towards the door.

— I've got a truth, she says.

— Great! Let's keep that for the next time we're at work, something to look forward to, I say.

Almost there, my hand is reaching out behind me for the handle…

— We don't work together anymore, she says.

— Of course, shit. I know, email me –

— My parents are away on holiday, she says, –You don't have to go.

A glacier moment. She stands and takes my hand and then through the hall and up the stairs and into her bedroom. Big, bigger than my whole flat probably, with the sort of double bed you only get in fancy hotels, fitted mirrored wardrobes. She takes her top off, and she's actually got great tits, and maybe there's still some E kicking about in my system not neutralised by all the booze because suddenly I'm getting turned on and kissing her as I'm trying to pull my jeans down. Make the mistake of seeing myself in the mirrors which is a complete passion killer but I look away quickly enough so the effect isn't terminal and now she's lying on the bed naked with her legs spread. She must be so into you Danny. Shit.

— You are really beautiful, I say.

— Fuck me Danny, she says.

— I want to, you can see for yourself, I really really want to but –

— But what? she says.

— Please don't cry, I say.

—I'm not going to cry, she says.

—I wasn't talking to you. Joanne, you're amazing and you saved me back there from those holiday snaps and for that I will be eternally grateful. Thing is though, I don't love you. I love someone else.

I try to give a little world weary smile and then realise I'm absently playing with myself, the animal part of my brain still focussed on the matter before me, and have to drop my hands quick and instead of what I hoped was an air of debonair despair I just look guilty as fuck.

—I love someone else too, she says.

This is painful, I say I love someone else and then she feels she has to say the same. The automatic teen response to everything. Phasers set to repeat. 'You're gay.' 'No you are.' 'I found a copy of Gay Cocksucker Monthly in your bag.' 'Gay Cocksucker Monthly doesn't even exist.' 'Yes it does, I've read it.' 'What you doing reading it? 'Looking at pictures of you.' And so on and so forth. Joanne hasn't closed her legs and I still have a rager which isn't helping. Best just to play along, the least I can do is help hide her embarrassment at being rejected.

—Who do you love? I say.

—Mark.

—Mark?

She nods. Fucking Mark!

—He's a complete arsehole, I say.

—No he's not.

Shouldn't let this get to me but can't help it.

—He's twice your age.

—So?

—Well, any guy over thirty that would go out with a teen-ager is dodgy as fuck. You hear them trying to justify themselves – *I only date younger girls because women my own age are all so bitter and cynical* – aye, that's cause bastards like you abused them when they were young.

She laughs but I can't stop, on a roll.

—And another thing, avoid any bloke that tries to get pity by saying 'Why don't women go out with nice guys? Nice guys like me.' Cause what he's really saying is why are women so stupid that they don't recognise how brilliant I am? Definite psychopath behaviour. And any guy that doesn't at least occasionally dabble with drink, drugs or gambling has got serious problems.

—So you're saying I should go out with an alcoholic, junkie, gambling addict?

—No of course not, just a man who can happily go through life without cutting loose at least now and again is not to be trusted.

—Thanks for the advice dad –

—I'm not finished! Workaholics, they're the biggest bastards of the lot, cause it's not enough that they want to spend every minute of the day in the office or making plans for world domination but they expect everyone else to be obsessed with the same nonsense they are. Seriously, Hitler, Stalin, Thatcher – too busy to sleep, those types – it's the workaholics that ruin everything for the rest of us.

She's laughing again, and it is at me but it's not vindictive because I think she thinks I'm putting on a performance for her. And in spite of everything I still have a hard-on, shit, she could be laughing at that.

—Wait a second, I say. —Getting back to Mark. If you love him why were you coming on to me tonight?

—To make him jealous.

Fucking unbelievable.

—Don't be upset, I like you too, Joanne says.

She sits up and takes my cock in her hand.

—Everything is about sex, apart from sex, which is about everything else, she says.

I nod but haven't a clue what she's talking about.

—Truth or dare, she says.

—I've never actually played this before–

—Sexually speaking, are you more sub or dom? she says.

And squeezes slightly.

—I'm classic switch, I say.

—What does that mean?

—I have no idea. I read it in *Farmer's Weekly*.

—Oh-oh, she says —Now it's a dare. Don't move.

Shouldn't it be my shot? I'm just about to start complaining because I'm still annoyed about the whole Mark thing but think, fuck it, it's a get out of jail free card, and then she takes me in her mouth and any doubts I had go out the window. She starts to use her hand as well and there's a few seconds of pure desperate overpowering need and then I orgasm and she quickly moves from my cock while I'm still cumming and kisses me, sticking her tongue in my mouth so I can taste it. When I open my eyes again I'm lying on the floor in the foetal position. How the fuck did I get there?

—Your turn, she says.

I uncurl myself and struggle to my knees.

—Whatever you want, I say.

She gets on the bed and positions herself on all fours.

—Fuck me, she says.

—I have just... y'know, so it might be some time.

—Fuck me, she says.

Right, move behind her and slip a couple of fingers inside and that's enough to trigger something cause I'm halfway hard again and then I don't need to use my fingers any more and we're fucking.

—Harder, she says.

—Yes, of course, I say.

—Harder.

Pick up the pace a bit but slightly worried about how recently I just came and I've heard stories about men tearing the cartilage in their penises.

—Harder!

—Yeah I heard you the first time, I say.

I should never have thought about breaking my dick because that's all I can think of now.

—Harder!

—I'm doing it as hard as I can. To be honest I'm amazed I'm doing this well.

Can feel myself deflate, shit, if I can somehow pull out and put my hand back in before she notices I can get away with this, the old Raiders Of The Lost Ark routine.

—Harder!

—I can't do it any harder! I say.

—Well use something else then, she says.

I stop.

—What?

—Use something else, she says.

And slide out of her.

—Something else? I say.

—In the drawer, there's a dildo, get it.

Too stunned to move. Is this how things are nowadays?

—What you waiting for?

I reach for the drawer and inside there is indeed the item in question. I pick it up.

—So just to clarify, I say. –What happens next?

—What do you think will happen? I'll use it. You can stay and watch if you like.

It's funny, normally the idea of a woman touching herself in front of me would be a real turn on but for some reason I feel like weeping. I give her the dildo and she gets to work. On the one hand, sex is the joining of souls – it's called making love because that's what it is – a celebration of the physical and spiritual that takes us to a place beyond human. And on the other hand there is fucking reality.

—You know what? I say, —I think I might just head off.

She doesn't ask me to stay and if I do I'm going to burst into tears so I seize the moment and run away. I know sex can't be amazing and mind blowing every time, but just once?

10

Awake. Need a slash but not getting up. If I forget about it I'll be able to go back to sleep. Forgetting about needing a piss is easier said than done. Not really hungover which is a surprise. Gotcha, I'm still drunk. Would explain the borderline cheerfulness. Should eat something while I can without bringing it straight back up, same with the trip to the toilet but know I'm going nowhere, not until actually wetting the bed is a genuine possibility. Conscious effort not to remember anything from last night and for once my memory does me a favour. Stole a bottle of whisky from Joanne's house on the way out and after that nothing. Was she lying about loving Mark? Was that an attempt to make me jealous? Oh God I hope not, cause then I was a right bastard. Fuck. Not your problem Danny. If you want to make yourself feel guilty about Joanne she can wait her turn. At least you got back home in one piece. Any night out you can walk away from is a good one. Got a restless buzz coming on. Maybe doing fuck all with your life isn't all it's cracked up to be. No, that's just the booze talking. I have my plan. Depression is anger turned in on itself. Like it's a bad thing. Better than some cunt running about shoving glasses in people's faces and pouring acid in the holes and shouting 'You wouldn't want me to be depressed, would you?' Jesus. The more anger directed inward the better. Ok, buzz has gone but still need the slash. If I'd gone as soon as I'd woken up I'd be back in bed by now and able to get to sleep. Or have a wank. But now having a wank will just make the desire to piss unbearable. Still... Let's get the right fantasy going and see what happens. Oh God, what if everybody you'd ever masturbated about knew? Cold sweat but not enough to put me off. Take a grip and I'm gonna pay for this later but fuck it –

    —Danny! I know you're in there. Open up. Seb's voice.

    —I'm not leaving until you see this!

I have to get up anyway for the slash so it might as well be now and as I make for the door I see the skull wearing a woolly hat set at a jaunty angle. I must have put that on it when I came in. No memory, that's a lie, a flash of me pouring it a drink and performing a ceremony, Christ, I think we're blood brothers. Shake myself.

    —Go away Seb. I'm not doing anything anymore. I told you that. You're not being fair.

    —Yeah, but check it out.

The letterbox rattles and a flyer falls onto the floor, landing blank side up.

    —What do you think?

Lean down and turn it over. The flyer. An advert. Picture of a big top, no don't, trapeze ahh please not today, lions and elephants on their hind legs, you fuckers and clowns. Clowns. The Circus. The fucking Circus. Circus. Fuckus. Cuntus. It never stops. It never bloody stops. I open the door. Paul's there as well.

    —You'd better come in.

    —What we gonna do about it? It opens tonight, Seb says.

—I don't make decisions anymore, I say. —That was the last decision I made and I'm sticking to it. I mess everything up, I'm man enough to accept that.

—But Danny. It's a fuckin' Circus, Seb says. —They need to be stopped, your words not mine.

And he's right. I may have hit that clown but they've still got one up on me. They had the last laugh. I must be drunk because one more time doesn't seem like too much.

—What's the plan then?

—I was thinking we could picket it tonight? That ok Danny?

—That's fine, but you shouldn't really be asking my opinion Seb. If this is a disaster all the responsibility is yours.

Paul points at the TV.

—Why have you got a skull?

—Oh that? It's nothing.

—Why is it wearing a hat?

—Cause you lose fifty per cent of body heat through your head.

Seb ignores the exchange between me and Paul. Good lad.

—Yeah, I can handle it, the responsibility, he says. —We'll pick you up and then head straight there. Alright?

I shrug. As if it makes a difference.

—Have you been talking to it? Paul says.

—Of course I've not been talking to it!

I take a step towards the skull and lift the headgear.

—The hat's off! Happy now?

Breathing heavily but he keeps on pushing me. Seb claps his hands.

—We should meet up earlier and make some placards.

—Yeah. I'm up for that, says Paul.

Shake my head and feel like giving them the vickies but don't bother. The door's still open and I usher them towards it.

— By the way, I'm taking the skull with me. Just to let you know, I say.

Seb nods.

— I kinda figured something like that, what with the hat an' all. Later Danny.

The door closes. Slash then wank then sleep. Doesn't work, the sleep part of it anyway. Put the telly on. *Back To The Future* is just starting and this is exactly what I need. Already getting drawn in and it's taking me out of myself and it's amazing how well it's put together... and then I make the mistake of thinking about the sequels which I made the mistake of watching which takes me back into myself, except it's worse than before because now as well as everything else I've got *Back To The Future 2* in my head. If they'd really needed a sequel they should have just rebooted the first one and made it with a high school girl instead of a boy. Wait a second, that's a terrible idea, because then it'd all be about her dad trying to get off with her and that's just creepy, so bad I have to switch it off. Well done Danny, you can never watch *Back To The Future* again without thinking of paedophilia. Don't start thinking of *It's A Wonderful Life*, I mean it, don't, wait a second, what if Clarence was actually working for the devil? That doesn't make any sense – yes it does, think about it – Clarence tried to kill himself, no angel would even pretend to do that, it's a mortal sin, he'd be damned for eternity. Dive under the covers. Shit. I need help or I'll never be able to watch a film ever again.

Maggie Shepherd's World Famous Circus. Faded Big Top, not

RAYMOND FRIEL

even that, just a large tent that could be army surplus. Rusty
waltzer with the obligatory dodgy looking geezers gazing on
from the sides, the definition of going nowhere fast. A merry-
go-round with the wooden horses badly chipped, more than
chipped, mutilated, fuckin' hell, one of them doesn't have a
face. Even by Circus standards this is poxy. Plus it's raining. We
don't need to be here, this place is on its last legs as it is. Seb's
proudly holding a placard with 'Just Say No *to Circuses*' on it,
but the last two words have been added recently in marker pen.

   —Did that used to be an anti-drugs thing?
Seb looks embarrassed.

   —Yeah, is it obvious?
I shake my head and let mine droop. It has a picture of an
elephant with some illegible words scrawled across it. Paul is
as chirpy as Seb, a poster with 'Stop This Animal Exploitation'
gripped his hands. A family – mum, dad and wee boy – pass. If
he's anything like I was he's about to have the shock of his life.
Seb rummages through a pile of black bags at his feet.

   —Danny, you ready to change sign? I made a 'Circus
   Maximus Crueltius' one especially for you, he says.
Slogans in Latin. That'll grab the common man's attention.

   —It's ok, I say, —This should do it.
I raise my 'fuck knows what it's supposed to be' high in the air.

   —Well tell me when you want to change, you too Paul, Seb
   says.
A woman smoking and pushing a pram passes without giving
us a look. Seb raises a megaphone to his lips.

   —It may look like the animals are having fun but they're
   not! It is only by beating them every day for years that they
   are terrorised into performing for you. This is no different

from bear baiting or dog fighting. Would you take your children to see that?

—Aye, I would! a young ned shouts.

He's dressed in a brown shell suit and with a lassie that could be his brother. God this is dire. Seb offers me the megaphone.

—You do it Danny, you're better than me.

—I told you Seb. I'm gonna stand here holding this and that's it. Don't ask me to do anything else cause I'm not gonna, ok?

He tries to hand the megaphone to Paul but he refuses and points to the hole in his cheek.

—I'd rather not draw attention to myself.

—Yeah. I understand.

Seb raises the megaphone to his lips

—Roll up! Roll up! If you like Circuses...

But he can't think of anything further to say and lowers the megaphone. That was practically an advertisement. I take a step back and my foot lands on something rubbery. Glance down. Big shoes. Don't look but can feel it, feel *him*, a presence. He's here. A clown. A fucking clown is standing right behind me. He shuffles to the side and stands just to my left. Full battle dress. Red nose, smeared make-up, orange wig. The smell of cheap wine. He's got his own sign, with 'Kick Me' plastered on it. Seb and Paul haven't noticed yet but I'm frozen and can't move. The clown sticks his chest out and gets a laugh from a group of teenagers entering. Seb finally gets it and turns round, seeing the clown.

—Just ignore him, Seb says.

Easier said than done when you got a bad dose of coulrophobia. Some people have stopped and are waiting for the show to begin.

I shouldn't have come here. I'm not ready for this. The clown parades up and down like a Sergeant Major. He stops in front of Paul and does an exaggerated double-take. He points at the wounded cheek, going up close and rubbing his eyes in disbelief. In a moment of inspiration he takes his red nose off and places it on his own cheek and hugs Paul as if they were long lost brothers. The crowd laughs and Paul's off, disappearing amongst the trailers. The clown bows to the audience and funny walks up to me. He stands like a statue and we all hold our breath. His flower sprays some water and it shoots onto my shoulder. He might as well be pissing on me.

—Danny, are you not going to do something? Seb says.
But it's not enough and I know I'm letting him down but just stand and take it anyway.

—I'm going to look for Paul, he says.
Seb ditches his placard and heads off. Just me and the clown. He makes a loud farting noise, wags his finger at me in disgust, and leaves while the crowd continues to laugh. His work here is done and I'm all alone. I should go, I really should, but even leaving's still doing something and nothingness is what I'm after. You can tell yourself things are going to change, you can tell yourself things are going to get better, but the truth is you are fucked. Only by accepting that fact can you move on. I'm a stone, a rock, part of the scenery. Aware of someone stopping in front of me but don't bother raising my head. At least it's not another clown, I would have seen the shoes by now. Get poked in the shoulder. I look up. It's Shona. She's dressed in dark green combat fatigues though no balaclava, which means I can see her face, but it doesn't give me the thrill it used to. I shake myself, suddenly feeling dizzy and sad but I smile for her anyway.

—Hey. You look nice. Softened it a bit.

—What you doing here Danny?

—Nothing.

—What's that supposed to mean?

—I'm just standing here. That's all. I'm not moving a muscle.

—Go home.

—Nope.

—Fine. But you'd better not get in the way.

She turns and starts to jog in the direction of the Big Top. Open the bag at my feet and pull out the skull.

—What am I supposed to do with this then?

That does the trick and she runs back to me.

—Put that thing away!

I do but can't help having a little laugh. So much for mini Celebrations or flowers, you want a woman's attention get yourself some incriminating evidence.

—What's wrong with you Danny?

Some questions it's best not to answer.

—Jason will take that off you later. Try not to lose it.

She turns her back on me and I'm a rock again. Unfeeling, unmoving, timeless. What's so great about being alive anyway? It's just long periods of monotony interspersed with short bursts of intense failure. Close my eyes and let time pass and it does. Don't know if I'm in the state just before sleep or just after. It's still raining and even though I'm wet I don't feel it. If there's anything closer to being dead I'd like to know what it is because this is brilliant. Bloody hell I think I'm meditating. Don't get excited Danny or you'll blow it. Level off. The abyss is your friend. Got to slow down on the inside as well. If Buddhist monks can lower their heartbeat by concentrating why not stop it altogether? Doesn't seem to be working. Concentrate harder. Shut my eyes tighter. That's enough heart, give it up. Feel my jaw muscles clenching. This isn't good. Heartbeat's gone up. Right ya cunt –

—Are you constipated?

Shona's voice. Open my eyes. She's back in front of me looking pretty wired, a black bin bag slung over her shoulder and sweat mixing with the rain on her face.

—No. Just thinking.

—Some thoughts you can do without.

She drops the bag at my feet amongst the others.

—You should move.

—No.

—Danny –

—Look Shona, so far tonight by not doing anything nothing bad has happened. My life choice has been vindicated and I'm hardly gonna change that after all this success, now am I?

—Keep it down Danny. You'll get us noticed.

—Well for fuckssake!

I hold up the sign.

—That's what I'm here for!

—Ok ok. I'll leave you to it. But if you're so happy not doing anything anymore, don't look in that bag.

I don't reply and she's off, running back towards the Circus. That little interchange slightly messed up my vegetable state but I can get it back. Take a deep breath and close my eyes again. Calm then death. What's in the bag? No, don't think like that, it's nothing to do with you. Something trickles down the back of my trousers and please God let it just be the rain. Come on

Danny, focus –

   —Danny!

It's Seb. At this rate I'll never stop my heart.

   —Can't you see I'm busy?

Paul's with him and seems to have calmed down a bit.

   —Something really weird is going on. We just saw that guy who was with Shona at the fox hunt lugging a fucking body bag about.

   —I saw it as well Danny, we gotta do something, Paul says.

   —No we don't. So what? Some guy's got a bag. We've all got bags with shit in them. I mean, Shona left one here a minute ago. It doesn't mean anything.

   —What bag?

   —Forget the bag. It doesn't matter. And anyway Paul, since when did you start caring about anything other than women?

I point at his face.

   —Honestly, how did that happen?

   —Danny we got other things to –

   —No. I want to hear the truth for a change. Paul, forgive me for being so blunt, but how the fuck did you end up with a hole in your face?

Paul looks at Seb for support and he nods at him to go for it.

   —… I was masturbating to some porn on the net and my semen hit the computer and there must have been electrical fault somewhere cause it blew up and a bit of the keyboard hit my face.

The worst thing is I'm not surprised.

   —But that's not important right now, Paul says.

   —You would say that, wouldn't you?

   —Danny, he's right, Seb says, –That isn't important right

now. Ok so he lied. We've all lied. I mean... I told Paul so I
suppose I'd better... and I tried to tell you before, but at the
start I only joined up because I was working on an article
about extremists. But then Danny you made me see that it
was worth fighting for. I'm sorry.

I fucking knew it. The corporate controlled press have been after
me all this time. And if they're in so are the security services.
Explains a lot. Thought I was getting paranoid but that old man
outside the B&Q was definitely at it. Or thought I was cruising.
Well well well. Can't help but feel proud and important. I must
have been doing something right after all.

—So what did those bastards give you for getting close to me?

—An A+.

—Eh?

—See that's another thing. I'm still at school. The article
was for my English class. Oh, and I live with my parents.
Not at the Commune.

—But we've talked for hours about life on the Commune!
Jesus Christ Seb, there was a time when I was seriously
thinking about joining you there (not true but still).

—I'm sorry Danny. I was embarrassed because you all had
your own places and were older than me.

Paul shakes his head, grinning.

—It's a bit of a laugh innit? Me pretending I'm younger
while Seb's pretending he's older.

And here I was thinking I was the odd one but it was those two
all along.

—Fantasy land. The pair of you.

They both lower their eyes.

—Sorry, Seb says.

—Yeah, sorry Danny.

—Should we all shake hands?

—It's ok Seb, we don't need to do that.

His face drops.

—No you're right. Let's all shake hands, I say.

One by one we squeeze each other's flesh.

—How about a group hug –

—That's enough Seb.

Paul points at the plastic bags at our feet.

—Which one did she leave?

I indicate it with my foot. Somehow it seems bigger than it did before.

—You know what Shona's like now. It could be anything. Maybe we should call the police? Paul says.

—No. I'll do it, I say.

Ok. The bag. What's the worst that can be in there? Another skull? Nothing to worry about. Right. Paul taps my shoulder.

—So you gonna look inside or –

—Give us a minute for fuckssake!

Paul makes a face at Seb as I lean down and poke my head in the bag. Hmm. Oh dear. Oh dear oh dear oh dear. This isn't good, oh no, this isn't good at all.

—What's in there? Seb says.

Can't answer can't breath can't do anything but something is building inside.

—C'mon Danny. Tell us.

Take my head out of the bag. Suck in oxygen. It's coming.

—Unbelievable. FUCKING UNBELIEVABLE! You saw me, I didn't do anything, I didn't do one fucking thing and yet I still end up with this shit.

—What is it?

—Take a fucking long shot. Another dead animal.

I pull the bag open and they see what I've seen, a Doberman with blood fresh from a blow to its head slumped lifeless and limp. I'm not putting up with this no fucking way. Sling the bag over my shoulder and start walking.

—Where you going? Seb says, looking scared.

—I'm gonna give it back to her.

—But Danny, there's something big going down –

—They'd better cancel it cause I've had enough.

Through the entrance and can hardly see. My chest is tightening and the only thing I can make out is the Big Top. The Big Top. Clown city. Cunt Shitty.

—Shona! Shona!

Calling her name but no idea if she can hear me. Something slaps against my ear and realise that the plastic bag has torn at the side and the dog's head has flopped out, banging against me every time I change direction.

—I got something for you Shona!

The bag tears and the Doberman falls onto the grass. Get on my hands and knees to pick it up and then she's in front of me.

—I've been looking for you, I say.

—You fuckin' idiot! Get up!

She grabs my hand but I pull it from her grasp and the momentum makes me fall back.

—I'll get up by myself.

—Get lost Danny. Believe me, I'm doing you a favour.

She's pissed off at me. *She's fucking pissed off at me?*

—I don't want any of your favours.

I point at the Doberman and even though I'm angry my voice is breaking.

　—You of all people should know that's gonna set me back a
　bit. I mean, fuckin' hell, it's another dead bloody dog.

Swallow and blink but can't stop the inevitable.

　—Don't break down on me Danny. The last thing I need
　right now is you getting hysterical.

Thanks a million love. Any sympathy and it would have been tears before bedtime but now death first.

　—You heartless bitch. This doesn't mean anything to you,
　does it?

I lift up the dog and put it in her face. She retreats.

　—Put that away.

She keeps backing off and I keep shoving it at her.

　—No, not until you've had a good look at it.

　—I don't want to –

And this time it's her voice that breaks. She stumbles and hits the ground. I drop the carcass onto her lap.

　—There you go. Merry fucking Christmas.

She hides her face and starts to cry. Good. About time… Shit.

　—You ok?

I sit beside her and take the Doberman from her lap and onto mine. She's crying and there's nothing to say. I put an arm around her and she lets it stay there as her whole body begins to shake. A few people pass but look away. Thank God for modern life's apathy and fear. I give her a squeeze.

　—This is really good for you. Keep it up.

Except it is and it isn't. Her cries have turned to shrieks and I can hear what's been locked up inside since the night on top of the research facility finally being unleashed because I've made the same noise myself. Cathartically fantastic but it's making a hell of a racket and at this rate we won't be ignored forever. I pat her on the back as the shrieks turn to screams.

　—This is great, I say. —I really mean that, but maybe we can do it somewhere else?

No change and I don't know what to do. Her voice alters and turns almost into a growl for a few seconds before hitting the high notes again. The family I saw earlier passes and the kid looks our way and I give him a smile and a wave but he looks freaked out. Something moves in my lap. The dog's head. It twitches and the eyes flick open. And then I'm on my feet and running about like a crazy person.

　—It's alive! That dog, that fucking dog is fucking alive!

Shona gets the message and through her tears starts to laugh. I lean down to stroke its head.

　—Ahh!

Bastard bites me. Fuckin' Dobermans. But it doesn't get a grip and keels over instead, still dazed from whatever happened to it in the first place. Whatever happened to it in the first place. That's still to be answered. Can see some Circus workers coming our way.

　—I think they want their dog back, I say.

Drag Shona to her feet.

　—We're leaving.

I take her hand and we're off, zigzagging through the trailers and even though they don't give chase we don't stop running till we've left the Circus far behind.

This is nice. Peace at last. Considering everything it could be a lot worse. Can still see the Big Top but at this distance it's festive not threatening. At least it's not cold and she's got her head on my shoulder which is the deal clincher. Don't blow it Danny, not this time.

—I'm sorry, she says.

—No need, I say.

You can talk all you like about the abyss, depression and the crisis of confidence in young men but if there's ever the chance of getting some action the world seems a helluva better place. And that's not as shallow as it sounds. She turns her head to look at me.

—I can't believe how mean I was to you. Why did you put up with it?

—Because you're my friend, I say.

She nods and smiles but her body shifts against me, lingers for a moment, and then moves away.

—You're my friend too, she says.

And the meaning couldn't be clearer. Friends. Just friends. Take in the view but am looking on the inside. It's not as bad as all that, I have a friend. Better than nothing, beats school I suppose. Feel her tense.

—What?

—Nothing.

She gets to her feet and looks in the direction of the Circus, chewing her lip.

—Tell me. What is it?

She gulps.

—They're going to fling her to the lions.

—Eh?

—Maggie Shepherd. The woman that runs the Circus. They're going to fling her to the lions.

Of course, makes sense, remain calm.

—Get tae fuck!

—Jason and a few of the others have been planning it for months. We'd already kidnapped her when I saw you. The Doberman was hers. It was trying to protect her.

More running but this time back towards the Circus. It's catching up with me, the lack of sleep and panic exercise. I must have lost weight. Through the entrance and not sure where we're going. Following Shona but she's almost as lost as I am. God these stalls are grotesque. Who would pay to come here? See Paul and Seb at a 'How hard can you punch?' machine.

—One of you phone the police.

—The pigs? What for?

—They're flinging Maggie Shepherd to the lions.

—What?

—Yeah, I know. Pretty far out.

Shona's vanishing into the crowd and I'm after her. Past the caravans with peeling paint to the cages at the back, out of sight of the paying customers. The stench of animal shit mixed with water. See a group of monkeys huddled together trying to keep warm. Maybe we should rethink about trying to save her. Shona slows down in front of me and hides against the side of a trailer. I join her. In front of us there's another cage, a sign with the words 'Lion Enclosure' on the side. Some fucking enclosure but they're there, not terribly healthy, somewhat cowed and miserable in the rain, but lions nonetheless. Two of them in a cage that shouldn't even hold one. Can make out Jason and a couple of other guys dressed in black, one of them working on the lock. At their feet a black body bag churns up the mud as it wriggles. The lions are at the back of the cage, as far away from the door as they can possibly be, cautiously waiting to see what happens next. Jason kneels down beside the bag and says something to it that I can't make out. Hear a click and the door opens. Jason rolls the bag into the cage. The lions remain where they are. The bag squirms again and one of the lions gets to his feet and sniffs the air.

—Go on. Get into her, Jason says.

But the lion sits back down beside its mate.

—Let's go, says the guy that opened the door.

—No! I want to see it eat her.

The other two head off leaving Jason on his own, his hands on the bars like so many fascinated spectators before him. The bag starts to worm across the cage floor in a blind attempt to escape but in reality headed straight for the corner where the lions have made their den. Even from where I am I can hear Jason's breathing speed up. Shona steps out of the shadows and I'm with her. He hears us and turns, relief replaced by anger. He points at me.

—I told you to get rid of him not bring him along.

—I know what you said but this is wrong. It isn't me.

A growl from inside the cage. The bag has crawled right in between the lions. One of them raises a paw and lightly cuffs it and the bag splits open, a sixty year-old woman with blood and mud on her face born again. Shona rushes in waving her hands and shouting but to no avail. Ok Danny, it's time. I step towards the cage – *Jesus they're big* – open the door – *there's fuckin' two of them* – and enter. Unzip my bag and pull out the Thirteenth Earl of Talbot's skull and whistle.

—Right guys that's enough, I say.

They prick their ears at the whistle and as I fling the skull to the

opposite corner of the cage the closest lion leaps and catches it
in mid air.

—Hey! That's my skull! Jason says.

And then a metallic click behind me. He wouldn't would he?
Grab the old woman and with Shona's help make it to the door.
The lions roar. No not like this. Who the fuck gets eaten by
lions nowadays? Push and pull but the door is locked. See Jason
moving past the caravans away from us. Oh shit.

—Open the door! Shona screams.

But he pays no heed and disappears into the night. Ok then.
Turn round to face the lions and they've just about finished
reducing the skull to dust. My hand looks for Shona's and she
meets me halfway. We grip each other tight.

—How did we get here? she says.

The question isn't how did we get here, it's never been how did
we get here. The question is, now that we're here, how the hell
are we going to get out? Their tails swish. Fucking lions man. I
don't want to die, I really don't, and it's not just the fear talking
either. Life could be good, I just need a bit more time to get
better at it.

—I think we've just been working through it, I say. —Pity it
came to this. Cause I feel a lot better now.

The lions crouch, preparing to spring.

—Back!

A word with the consistency of treacle comes from the old
woman at our feet. The lions react as if struck and cower, slink-
ing their way back to the far end of the cage with their tails
between their legs, the memory of pain more powerful than the
lure of fresh food. Know that she probably just saved our lives
but what a fucking bitch this Maggie Shepherd must be to instil

such fear. She's trying to stand and practically crawls up my body to get to her feet, Jesus, apart from the humiliation with Joanne, that's the most female contact I've had in over a year.

    —It's alright. Don't move. I'm getting you out, a man says behind me.

Turn and see a clown, the same borderline child-abusing bastard who was fucking with us earlier, at the lock. There's already a bit of a crowd with more joining every second which is strange because five seconds ago I could have sworn that it was only me and Shona left in the whole planet. Paul and Seb are there too, looking frightened and out of place. The cage door swings open. Hands grab me but I push them off to have one last look at the lions. On both of them their ribs are showing and their fur's matted and littered with bald spots, grey and red itchy skin visible underneath. That motherfucking bitch. Can feel burning inside. Maggie rests her hands on my shoulder and stands tall, clearing her throat. It's only now I realise she's dressed ready to go on stage, black trousers and red tails. Sense the audience, an equal mix of Circus workers and civilians, are in awe of her and expect a performance. She extends her hand and someone gives her a top hat which she puts on with a flourish. Fucking hell.

    —Ladies and Gentleman, she says.

And smiles at me and Shona.

    —If you could kindly give three cheers for my rescuers –

    —Fuck off! I shout.

Thank God it's back. I thought it was gone but it was there all along. Maggie stops speaking and I shrug off her hand.

    —Youse are all cunts, I say.

The crowd that was ready to clap falls silent. I see Paul next to a huge bastard waving at me to stop. No way. I point at the lions.

—You should be ashamed of yourselves, the lot of you.
I glance at Shona who looks as angry as I am.

—If she hadn't have been in there I wouldn't have lifted a
finger to save this old bag, I say.
Well that's ruined a Kodak moment. The crowd is getting uglier
which is saying something when it comes to carny folk.

—And we'll be back tomorrow night protesting about this.
We're gonna shut you down, Shona says.
She takes my hand and we have to barge our way through the
mob. See the clown again and try to fling a punch but there's too
many bodies in the way and end up hitting a woman (trapeze
artist?) on the back of the head by accident and then we're free,
heading away from the Circus with Paul and Seb at our side.
Take the time to look at Shona and don't care if she's aware
I'm doing it or not. Friends. I can accept that, it's good, not a
disappointment, just for the millions of other things I need I'll
have to go somewhere else. I'm twenty two, I'm a man, and
ready for a proper relationship…
To hell with it.
Fuck the landlord.
I'm getting a pet.

The End

Some other books published by **LUATH** PRESS

Monks

Des Dillon
ISBN 978 1905222 75 9 PBK £7.99

Three men are off from Coatbridge to an idyllic Italian monastic retreat in search of inner peace and sanctuary.

... like hell they are. Italian food, sunshine and women – it's the perfect holiday in exchange for some easy construction work at the monastery.

Some holiday it turns out to be, what with optional Mass at 5am, a mad monk with a ball and chain, and the salami fiasco – to say nothing of the language barrier.

But even on this remote and tranquil mountain, they can't hide from the chilling story of Jimmy Brogan. Suddenly the past explodes into the present, and they find more redemption than they ever bargained for.

This story... is simultaneously hilarious and touching, morose and vividly energetic, but it is the seamless juxtaposition of the protagonists' internal and external worlds, added to the wonderfully wacky, frenetic narrative, that gives it its fire.
THE HERALD

The Glasgow Dragon

Des Dillon

ISBN 978-1842820-56-8 PBK £9.99

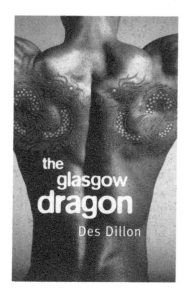

What do I want? Let me see now. I want to destroy you spiritually, emotionally and mentally before I destroy you physically.

When Christie Devlin goes into business with a triad to take control of the Glasgow drug market little does he know that his downfall and the destruction of his family is being plotted. As Devlin struggles with his own demons the real fight is just beginning.

Nothing is as simple as good and evil. Des Dillon is a master storyteller and this is a world he knows well.

Des Dillon's turn at gangland thriller is an intelligent, brutal and very Scottish examination of the drug trade.
THE LIST

Des Dillon writes like a man possessed. The words come tumbling out of him. ...His prose... teems with unceasing energy.
THE SCOTSMAN

Me and Ma Gal

Des Dillon

ISBN 978-1-842820-54-4 PBK £5.99

If you never had to get married an that I really think that me an Gal'd be pals for ever. That's not to say that we never fought. Man we had some great fights so we did.

A story of boyhood friendship and irrepressible vitality told with the speed of trains and the understanding of the awkwardness, significance and fragility of that time. This is a day in the life of two boys as told by one of them, 'Derruck Danyul Riley'.

Dillon's book is arguably one of the most frenetic and kinetic, living and breathing of all Scottish novels... The whole novel crackles with this verbal energy.

THE LIST 100 Best Scottish Books of All Time, 2005

Six Black Candles

Des Dillon

ISBN 978-1-906307-49-3 PBK £8.99

'Where's Stacie Gracie's head?'
... sharing space with the sweetcorn
and two-for-one lemon meringue
pies... in the freezer.

Caroline's husband abandons
her (bad move) for Stacie Gracie,
his assistant at the meat counter,
and incurs more wrath than he
anticipated. Caroline, her five
sisters, mother and granny, all
with a penchant for witchery,
invoke the lethal spell of the six
black candles. A natural reaction
to the break up of a marriage?

The spell does kill. You only have
to look at the evidence. Mess
with these sisters, or Maw or Oul
Mary and they might do the six
black candles on you. But will
Caroline's home ever be at peace
for long enough to do the spell
and will Caroline really let them
do it?

Set in present day Irish Catholic
Coatbridge, *Six Black Candles*
is bound together by the ropes
of traditional storytelling and
the strength of female familial
relationships. Bubbling under
the cauldron of superstition,
witchcraft and religion is the
heat of revenge; and the love and
venom of sisterhood.

A great dramatic situation, in which
the primitive Darwinian passions
of lust, rage, vengeance, and fierce
family loyalty come into conflict
with the everyday scepticism of the
sisters' modern lives. Dillon spins
physical and verbal comedy out of
his scenario with all the flair of a
born playwright.
THE SCOTSMAN

The writing is always truthful,
immediate and powerful.
SCOTLAND ON SUNDAY

They Scream When You Kill Them

Des Dillon
ISBN 978-1-905222-35-3 PBK £7.99

From pimps to Shakespeare, langoustines to lurchers Dillon's short stories bite... hard. Welcome to Dillon's world; a world where murderous poultry and evolutionary elephants make their mark. Des takes you from the darkness of *The Illustrated Man* and *Jif Lemons* to the laugh out loud *Bunch of C****.*

These stories are instantly accessible and always personal. Relationships and places and language are set precisely with few words and no flinching. If you're an alcoholic, recovering alcoholic, insane, a policeman, prisoner, gold digger, farmer, animal lover, Scots Irish or Irish Scots you may well recognise yourself somewhere in this book.

A brilliant storyteller of his own people, of all people.
LESLEY RIDDOCK

... raw, exciting Dillon with his taut use of language and a racy approach to literature and ideas, sometimes verging on the bizarre... as irresistible as ever.
DGB LIFE

... collecting it all together enhances the reputation he's established with novels like Me and Ma Gal *and* Six Black Candles, *and highlights what an asset we have in Des Dillon.*
THE GUIDE

My Epileptic Lurcher

Des Dillon

ISBN 978 1906307 74 5 PBK £7.99

The incredible story of Bailey, the dog who walked on the ceiling; and Manny, the guy who got kicked out of Alcoholics Anonymous for swearing.

Manny is newly married, with a puppy, a flat by the sea, and the BBC on the verge of greenlighting one of his projects. Everything sounds perfect. But Manny has always been an anger management casualty, and the idyllic village life is turning out to be more *League of Gentlemen* than *The Good Life*. As his marriage suffers under the strain of his constant rages, a strange connection begins to emerge between Manny's temper and the health of his beloved Lurcher.

It's one of the most effortlessly charming books I've read in a long time.
SCOTTISH REVIEW OF BOOKS

Help Me Rhonda

Alan Kelly

ISBN 978-1-905222-83-1 PBK £9.99

Rhonda. The answer's Rhonda.
I hate Rhonda. Hate her with a passion.
A desire. I love to hate her.

Sonny Jim McConaughy is no stranger to trouble. He blackmails his lawyer, scams the insurance company, drinks, takes drugs and sleeps around.

However, Sonny Jim has stumbled in to more trouble than even he can handle, waking up to find himself accused of attempted murder with no memory of the previous drunken night. So his girlfriend Rhonda, determined to stop them destroying them both, pits herself against him in a desperate battle of attrition.

A book to make you laugh and cringe throughout, filled with grit, realism, dark humour and a hilarious cast of misfits.

... shares a flare for the colourful language and violent scenarios of the Trainspotting scribe.
THE EVENING TIMES

Writing in the Sand

Angus Dunn

ISBN 978-1-905222-91-2 PBK £8.99

At the furthest end of the Dark Island lies the village of Cromness, where the normal round of domino matches, meetings of the Ladies' Guild and twice-daily netting of salmon continues as it always has done. But all is not well. Soon the characters are involved in a battle to either save or destroy the Dark Isle. But are they truly aware of the scale of events? And who will prevail?

It is a latter day baggy monster of a novel... a hallucinogenic soap... the humour at first has shades of Last of the Summer Wine, *alternating with* The Goons *before going all out for the* Monty Python meets James Bond, *and don't-scrimp-on-the-turbo-charger method... You'll have gathered by now that this book is a grand read. It's an entertainment. It alternates between compassionate and skillful observations, elegantly expressed and rollercoaster abandonment to a mad narrative.*
NORTHWORDS NOW

A gold, confident debut, packed to the gunnels with memorable characters and wry humour.
THE LIST

This Road is Red

Alison Irvine

ISBN 978 1906817 81 7 PBK £7.99

It is 1964. Red Road is rising out of the fields. To the families who move in, it is a dream and a shining future.

It is 2010. The Red Road Flats are scheduled for demolition. Inhabited only by intrepid asylum seekers and a few stubborn locals, the once vibrant scheme is tired and out of time.

Between these dates are the people who filled the flats with laughter, life and drama. Their stories are linked by the buildings; the sway and buffet of the tower blocks in the wind, the creaky lifts, the views and the vertigo. This Road is Red is a riveting and subtle novel of Glasgow.

One of the most important books about Glasgow and urban life I've read in a very long time. It offers an insight into city life that few Scottish novels can emulate.
PROFESSOR WILLY MALEY

Hand for a Hand

Frank Muir

978-1906817-51-0 PBK £6.99

An amputated hand is found in a bunker, its lifeless fingers clutching a note addressed to DCI Andy Gilchrist. The note bears only one word: Murder.

When other body parts with messages attached are discovered, Gilchrist finds himself living every policeman's worst nightmare – with a sadistic killer out for revenge.

Forced to confront the ghosts of his past, Gilchrist must solve the cryptic clues and find the murderer before the next victim, whose life means more to Gilchrist that his own, is served up piece by slaughtered piece.

Hand for a Hand is the second in Frank Muir's DI Gilchrist series.

A bright new recruit to the swelling army of Scots crime writers.
QUINTIN JARDINE

Luath Press Limited
committed to publishing well written books worth reading

LUATH PRESS takes its name from Robert Burns, whose little collie Luath (*Gael.*, swift or nimble) tripped up Jean Armour at a wedding and gave him the chance to speak to the woman who was to be his wife and the abiding love of his life. Burns called one of 'The Twa Dogs' Luath after Cuchullin's hunting dog in Ossian's *Fingal*. Luath Press was established in 1981 in the heart of Burns country, and now resides a few steps up the road from Burns' first lodgings on Edinburgh's Royal Mile.
Luath offers you distinctive writing with a hint of unexpected pleasures.

Most bookshops in the UK, the US, Canada, Australia, New Zealand and parts of Europe either carry our books in stock or can order them for you. To order direct from us, please send a £sterling cheque, postal order, international money order or your credit card details (number, address of cardholder and expiry date) to us at the address below. Please add post and packing as follows: UK – £1.00 per delivery address; overseas surface mail – £2.50 per delivery address; overseas airmail – £3.50 for the first book to each delivery address, plus £1.00 for each additional book by airmail to the same address. If your order is a gift, we will happily enclose your card or message at no extra charge.

Luath Press Limited
543/2 Castlehill
The Royal Mile
Edinburgh EH1 2ND
Scotland
Telephone: 0131 225 4326 (24 hours)
Fax: 0131 225 4324
email: sales@luath.co.uk
Website: www.luath.co.uk